**Michelle Kwan
presents**

Skating Dreams

Staying Balanced

Read all the *Skating Dreams* books!

Coming soon . . .

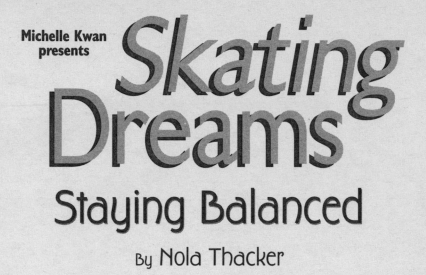

Michelle Kwan
presents

Skating Dreams

Staying Balanced

By Nola Thacker

Hyperion Paperbacks for Children

New York

Printed in the United States of America
First edition
1 3 5 7 9 10 8 6 4 2
This book is set in 12.5-point Life.
ISBN: 0-7868-1380-6
Visit www.hyperionchildrensbooks.com

1

“No, no, no!”

Lauren Wing stopped what she was doing. She bent over, put her hands on her knees, and took a deep, ragged breath. The cold burned her nose and eyes.

She straightened and looked in the direction of her new skating coach. Tiny, imposing Eve Perry in her bright yellow jacket seemed to fill the far end of the Silver Springs Skating Rink. Coach Perry raised one bare hand and beckoned for Lauren to come to her.

I will not cry, thought Lauren, scrubbing the back of one glove across her eyes. There. That was better.

But it bothered Lauren that an ordinary correction from the coach made her feel like crying. She couldn't blame Coach Perry. It wasn't her fault.

Coach Perry wasn't mean. She never shouted or lost her temper as Lauren knew some figure skating coaches did. She merely insisted on perfection and had an eagle eye for the tiniest mistake. But that was one of the things Lauren liked about the coach. Lauren herself never wanted to do anything less than perfectly.

It was, after all, the only way to be the best—and Lauren Wing wanted to be the best figure skater in the world.

Shake it off, Lauren told herself as she glided back down the ice toward Eve. It's just early and you're a little tired, maybe. You're having a bad-feeling morning.

"Do you feel it? That bad feeling?" asked Eve, as Lauren glided to a halt next to the coach. For a startled moment, Lauren thought the coach had read her mind. But then Eve reached out and caught Lauren's hand, pulling her arm out straight. She positioned Lauren's other arm behind her. "You are off balance," Eve said. "Your arms are out of position." She gave the back arm a little push to demonstrate, and even standing still, Lauren almost fell.

Coach Perry went on, "And if you are off balance, whatever you do will look clumsy, even if you don't fall."

Lauren tried holding her arms in a slightly different position. They felt like someone else's arms, stuck to her body.

"Inside, first." The coach tapped her chest with the tips of two bright red fingernails. "You must be balanced inside first, and then it will show on the outside."

Closing her eyes, Lauren tried to feel the balance her coach was talking about. Coach Perry talked about balance more than anything else in her lessons. Lauren knew how important it was. But inside, she felt nothing.

"You must feel as if you are part of the ice," Eve said. "You cannot fight against it."

"I know," Lauren said softly. She opened her eyes and gave her coach a quick, stiff-lipped smile.

The coach touched one of Lauren's fingertips. Although she always came to these dawn practices bundled up in hat, scarf, coat, and leg warmers over thick tights, and skate warmers over her skates, Coach Perry never wore gloves at practice, no matter how cold the ice was inside the rink. She had small, quick hands, and she wore colorful nail polish that she seemed to change almost as often as she changed clothes.

"Find the balance," Coach Perry said.

Today Lauren was wearing her fingerless gloves, and the coach's hand felt warm to her numb fingers.

Coach Perry frowned as she never frowned, even when Lauren made big mistakes while practicing. "You're cold," she said. "Balance and cold do not go together. We'll take a break so that you can drink something hot and put on warmer gloves."

"I don't . . ." Lauren began. She was going to say that she didn't have any extra gloves with her that day, but Coach didn't wait to listen.

Skating to the rink's edge, Coach Perry leaned over and lifted an enormous tote bag

4

from behind the boards. Balancing the bag on the railing, she rummaged through it, then produced a pair of red mittens patterned with white snowflakes and brought them to Lauren.

Lauren had been watching in fascination. The coach's tote bag was a mystery, a sort of Aladdin's treasure chest—Lauren could never guess what Eve would take out of it next.

"First the mittens," the coach said. "Then the hot cocoa."

"Hot cocoa?" asked Lauren.

"The mittens," Coach Perry said sternly.

Lauren put on the mittens. Satisfied, the coach reached back into her mystery bag and took out a silver thermos. She poured hot cocoa into the cup and handed it to Lauren.

The steam warmed Lauren's nose and cheeks. For a moment, she felt the way she had when she was little kid who had been out on a frozen pond ice skating all day. She smiled at the memory of chasing her older brother, Bryan, as his big feet in their black hockey skates flashed just ahead of her. "Catch me," he would call. "Come on, Lauren, you can do it!"

Bryan had played that game with Lauren, and then with Lacey Wing, their younger sister, who was eight. Soon he would play it with five-year-old Lisa, their youngest sister.

I think that's when I first began to love the ice, thought Lauren. She finished her hot cocoa and raised her eyes to meet Coach Perry's.

The coach smiled one of her quick smiles. "There," she said. "Better?"

"Better," agreed Lauren, handing the cup back to the coach.

"From the beginning," the coach decided. "We have time."

Lauren skated back out to center ice. She raised her hand and pushed off. Stroke, stroke, stroke, lean. Jump. Spin. Motions she'd done a million times before came to her as naturally as breathing. The ice was no longer her enemy. She forgot about the cold.

She finished in triumph, and flashed a judge-worthy smile over at her coach.

"Ah," said Coach Perry. "Practice and a little hot cocoa . . . much better. We'll stop now."

Still smiling, Lauren skated off the ice. She

liked finishing practice this way, having done her best and won her coach's approval. "Much better" from Eve was like some people shouting "Bravo!" and leaping to their feet with wild applause.

The glow of happy satisfaction stayed with Lauren as she got ready for school in the Silver Springs locker room. She stowed the gear that she kept at the rink in her locker and looked around the room. It was still hard to believe that she was part of the big, new rink, a sponsored member, taking lessons from one of the best coaches in the world of figure skating. Everything had happened so fast. One minute, she'd been one of many skaters at the Pine Creek Skating Rink in her hometown of Pine Creek in the Adirondack mountains of New York, and the next minute, she was being invited to be Coach Perry's new student.

And Lauren's dream, that secret, shining dream of one day skating in the Olympics, had suddenly seemed a little closer, a little more real.

She smiled and closed the locker door and locked it. She was the luckiest girl in the world.

Her mother returned her smile as Lauren ran lightly down the steps of the rink and up to the van and opened the door. "Good practice?" she asked.

"The best," she answered. She got inside and buckled her seat belt. The almost silent, still, silver-gray dawn in which she had arrived at the rink had given way to sunlight and the noise of traffic and the bustle of people on the streets of Saratoga Springs. She watched a pair of students, their backpacks bulging with books, as they pushed into a coffee shop. College students, she guessed. Maybe they'd been up all night long, studying for a test.

I should be studying for my math test, Lauren thought suddenly. She'd almost forgotten about it.

Lauren wished she *could* forget the test. She'd studied a little the night before, but when her yawns had started adding up more than her equations had, she'd decided she would study the next morning on the way to the rink. The trip from Pine Creek to Saratoga Springs took almost an hour each way. She would have plenty of time to make herself test-proof.

But she'd fallen asleep on the way to her lesson that morning, as she often did.

Now, as the van turned onto the highway, Lauren reached into her backpack and pulled out her math book and her notebook. She rifled through the pages. She picked up her pencil. The numbers danced in front of her eyes.

Concentrate, she told herself. She did one problem. She did another. She stopped to think. Her eyelids drooped, snapped up, drooped again. Her head tipped sideways and came to rest on the window. Lauren quickly fell asleep.

She woke with a start as the van eased to stop. "We're here, sleepyhead," her mother said.

"Here?" Lauren croaked. "School?" She sat bolt upright.

The familiar brick building loomed as large as a nightmare in front of her.

"It looks like your school," said her mother. "I'm pretty sure we're in the right place." She grinned at her. "Hope the beauty sleep helped."

"Why didn't you wake me?" Lauren wailed.

Her mother's grin faded. "A little extra sleep never hurts, especially with your schedule. . . . Is something wrong?"

Lauren's thoughts flew. The test! How could she have slept? What was she going to do? What if she failed?

But she couldn't tell her mother. She might say the morning lessons were too much. She might make her stop skating.

Her mother said, "Lauren?"

Lauren forced herself to smile. "Everything's fine, Mom. I just wanted to do a little extra studying. But it's no problem."

"You're sure?"

"Absolutely positively triple-flip sure," Lauren assured her, borrowing a phrase from Annie, one of her skating buddies. "See you tonight."

To Lauren's relief, the worried look left her mother's face. "All right then. Have a good day," she said.

"You, too," she said as she hastily stuffed her books in her backpack and slid out of the car.

Then Lauren whirled in a near-perfect spin,

minus the ice, and raced through the students gathering on the steps. She still had a few minutes before her first class. She'd have to cram. She was skating on thin ice!

2

"How'd you do?" Rebecca Meyers asked as Lauren came out of her math class. She was standing just outside the classroom door, leaning with her oversized red bike-messenger bag she always carried.

Lauren groaned and made a gagging sound.

"Uh-oh," said Rebecca. She let out a little puff of breath that made her bangs flutter above her dark eyebrows.

"I need some water," Lauren said. "And a new brain."

"The water I can help you with," Rebecca said, leading the way down the hall to the water fountain.

Lauren took a long drink of the cold water. Why did tests make her so thirsty? When she'd finished, she straightened and sighed.

"About that new brain," Lauren said, trying to make a joke of it.

Rebecca pretended to look into her messenger bag. "Nope. Sorry. Must have left that extra one at home."

"Too bad," Lauren said. "I could have used one—even a cat's brain."

"Cats don't worry about math tests," Rebecca said. Rebecca loved cats. An only child, she shared her house with her parents—and seven cats—and two dachshunds. Lost, hurt, or homeless cats had a way of finding the Meyerses, and the Meyerses had a way of finding good homes for many of those same cats.

Lutz, the Wings' cat, who slept on Lauren's bed most nights, had been found by Rebecca. Rebecca had found him one winter day in third grade on the way home from school, a scrawny, dirty gray kitten hiding under a car. With Lauren's help, she'd coaxed the wary scrap of fur out, wrapped him in her jacket and Lauren's muffler, and taken him home.

Lauren named him and adopted him. The skittish kitten grew into a sleek silver tomcat. Lutz was the best present Rebecca had ever given her.

"So," Rebecca said. "That test wasn't so bad."

"Well," said Lauren, "I don't know. But I don't *think* so."

Lauren's doubt stopped Rebecca in her tracks. "Lauren! Are you serious?"

"You've never flunked a test in your life. Never!" Rebecca exclaimed. Rebecca knew what she was talking about. Rebecca and Lauren had been best friends since first grade, when they had both had a crush on Randy Bishop and had had a fight over who was going to choose him for the kickball team.

"I've never flunked a test." Lauren groaned.

"Lauren?" Rebecca's voice was anxious.

"More water," Lauren managed to choke out, and practically dove into the fountain. Coming up for air, she splashed a few drops onto her hot cheeks and burning eyes. There. She was in control now.

"If you failed the test," Rebecca persisted, "won't you have to stop skating or something? I mean, isn't that what your parents said?"

"They said I had to keep my grades up. One low grade on a test doesn't mean I'll get a low grade for the term. It's just one test." Lauren spoke more sharply then she had intended. She bit her lip and went on in a calmer tone, "I'll do better on the next test. I'll ace it."

"But . . ." Rebecca said.

"We're here," Lauren said. Language arts was the one class Lauren and Rebecca still had together. In order to take the early morning lessons at Silver Springs, the only time that the ice and Coach Perry were free, Lauren had had to rearrange her schedule at school. The school had agreed to count her first period of the day as study hall and to allow her to skip both it and homeroom, which took place while she was in the van riding back from her lesson.

Now, except on Tuesdays, Lauren's school day began when she checked into the office before second period and headed straight to class. But not having study hall was harder than

Lauren had thought. And she missed being in homeroom and math with Rebecca.

She glanced over at Rebecca. "Forget the math," she said in a low voice, as the last of the students shuffled into the room. "I've got a more important number in mind. Like, eleven?"

For a moment, Rebecca's forehead creased in a puzzled frown. Then laughter lit her gray eyes. "My birthday!" she said.

Lauren smiled and nodded. The distraction had worked. "Anybody getting the hints?" she asked.

"Well, I opened all the magazines in the house to pages that had nice pictures of computers," said Rebecca. "And I've mentioned a *few* times that my computer's name is 'Dinosaur.'"

"Subtle," said Lauren. Rebecca wanted a new computer for her birthday. Lauren didn't understand it, but if that's what Rebecca really wanted, Lauren was ready to cheer her on.

"Yeah," said Rebecca. "I'm not sure it's working, though. I may have to have a *serious* talk with my dad."

Mrs. Campbell cleared her throat. "Rebecca,

Lauren, if you're ready, we'll start class."

"Okay, Mrs. Campbell," Rebecca said. She flashed Lauren a talk-to-you-later grin.

Lauren nodded, tapped her watch, and spread her hands out wide. Then she held her thumb to her ear and her little finger by her mouth. That meant "I'll call you tonight." Rebecca nodded back and opened her book.

Lauren swallowed a yawn. She'd stay after school in the school library to study, until it was time to go to the Pine Creek Skating Rink to practice. Then she'd go home, set the table for dinner, throw her skating gear into the laundry, and start a load before her parents got home. If there was time, she would study some more before dinner. And she'd definitely have to do some major page turning in math and science after dinner. Calling Rebecca would be the treat at the end of a long day.

Lauren stepped out onto the ice and stopped at the sight of two rear ends facing her. "This is *not* polite," she said.

Annie McGrath and Danielle Kurowicki

straightened up and Annie cried, "Lauren!" as if she hadn't seen Lauren for days, when they had practiced together only the day before. "We were just doing some warm-up stretches."

Danielle said, "You're so *late*. We thought you'd been in a traffic accident. Or a bank robbery, maybe."

"I'm just five minutes late," Lauren protested. "And what would I be doing in a bank?"

"You could have been riding by and noticed something suspicious," Danielle said. "And while you were calling the police, the driver of the getaway car saw you and knew he had to stop you. So he jumped out of the car and you . . ."

"Danielle!" Lauren held up her hand.

"Well, it could have happened that way," argued Danielle.

"I was *studying*. At the school library," Lauren said. "No bank robbers. Not even an overdue book. And you could have started practice without me."

"Nah," said Annie. She bent down again, touching the tips of her skates with her mittens.

Danielle did the same and Lauren joined them. She took deep breaths and tried to relax, to make her muscles long and loose. Stretching was an important part of avoiding injury and staying balanced. If you were balanced, you were less likely to get injured—and Lauren couldn't afford to get injured.

A few minutes later, she stepped onto the ice and began to warm up with slow, easy strokes. The rink was crowded with the skaters who came for the free skating period, and Lauren had to keep a sharp eye out for zigzagging kids and ankle-turning beginners.

After the third circle, Lauren leaned forward, extended her arms like wings, and lifted her back skate up. Behind her, she knew that Annie and Danielle were doing the same. It was their follow-the-leader warm-up, their shadow skating drill. Each of them would take the lead for one lap around the rink, striking different poses and doing various moves for the others to imitate.

Danielle's finale made both Lauren and Annie laugh. Tall, with long legs and graceful arms, Danielle had chosen a dramatic, dying swan move for her last pose as leader of the shadow skating drill. She'd thrown one arm across her forehead and pressed the other hand to her heart, her eyes almost closed, her expression tragic.

Giggling and struggling to hold the pose, the three friends glided to a halt at rink side.

"If you don't keep skating, Danielle," Lauren said, "you're going to be a very famous movie star."

Danielle looked pleased. "You think?" Then her face grew serious. "But I'd rather skate. *Anybody* can be a movie star."

"Not anybody," a familiar voice drawled.

Danielle, Annie, and Lauren stopped talking. Silently, sneakily, Erica Claiborn had somehow suddenly appeared on the ice next to them.

"You have to have looks. And talent," Erica continued. She smirked at Danielle. "But then, you have to have talent for skating, too. Maybe you should consider some *other* career, Danielle."

Annie's brown eyes snapped and her quick temper flared. Lauren put her hand on Annie's arm as Annie struggled to keep from exploding with indignation.

Danielle's round cheeks flushed, but she held on to her composure. Taking one step closer to Erica, Danielle looked at the other girl for a long moment. They were both tall, about the same height, with a similar grace. But Erica's short, smooth brown hair and calculating blue eyes contrasted sharply with Danielle's dandelion explosion of blond curls and her expressive hazel eyes.

As the two girls faced each other, Lauren wondered for about the millionth time why Erica was so nasty to everybody. After all, Erica had everything she wanted: new skating costumes for practically every competition, private lessons with Coach Knudson at the Pine Creek rink, a family with plenty of money to pay for new skates and new blades whenever Erica needed them.

All of these were things that Lauren's family couldn't afford. Her own skates were held together with polish, tight lacing, and extra stitching to make them last as long as possible.

Her mother made all of Lauren's costumes. And the only reason Lauren had been able to accept Coach Perry's invitation to study with her was because her whole family watched every penny that they spent.

Just when Lauren thought Danielle and Erica might stand nose-to-nose forever, Danielle spoke. "Thank you, Erica. I'm sure your opinion is valuable to somebody. You can go now. My friends and I are busy."

"Oh, I'm wounded," Erica shot back sarcastically. She spun and sped away with a flip of the skirt on her expensive, perfectly matched skating outfit.

"Wow," said Annie. "I would have totally gone nuts on her. But you were so . . . calm, Danielle."

"I was pretending I was a great movie star in a big hotel and Erica was from room service," Danielle explained seriously. Then she grinned as her two friends went off into whoops of laughter.

And, for a moment, laughing with her skating buddies, Lauren forgot all her math troubles.

3

"*Aaaaahhhhh!*"
The scream jolted Lauren from her desk. Her pen slid across the book report she'd been writing and left a line of blue ink.

"*AAAAAAHHHH!*"

Leaping to the door of the bedroom she shared with her two sisters, Lauren stuck her head out into the hall. "Lisa?" she asked. "Is that you? What's wrong?"

Lauren's youngest sister, who was five, came racing down the hallway, her eyes bright and her cheeks red. "Save me, save me, save me!" she shrieked.

"Me, too!" shouted eight-year-old Lacey,

who was right behind Lisa. Lisa dodged one way around Lauren and into the bedroom. Lacey dodged the other.

But Lacey didn't make it.

Bryan, their fourteen-year-old brother, grabbed the back of Lacey's red sweatshirt and held on. "Fee, fi, fo, fum, I smell the blood of Lacey Wing," he chanted in a gruff voice.

Laughing and struggling, Lacey said, "Okay, okay. I surrender."

"Then it's your turn to be the Billy Goat Gruff," said Bryan in his normal voice.

Lisa peeped out from around Lauren. "Can I come out?" she whispered.

"It's safe," Lauren said. "The goat caught Lacey."

"Oh, good," said Lisa.

"You just wait," said Lacey. She growled at Lisa, and Lisa gave another shriek of mock terror and dodged behind Lauren again.

"Come play, come play," Lisa begged, as Lacey went down the hall toward the bathroom, chanting 'Fe, fi, fo, fum' under her breath.

But Lauren shook her head regretfully. "I

can't. I still have a report to write and I need to do some catch-up studying."

Looking smug, Bryan said, "I finished *my* homework."

"Me, too," said Lisa.

"You don't have homework," Lauren told her youngest sister. "You're in kindergarten."

"I did too have homework," Lisa said indignantly. "I had to draw a picture of my favorite animal. I drew Lutz. Want to see?"

"Sorry," Lauren said. "Not right now."

"Fe, fi, fo, fum!" Lacey called. "Ready or not, here I come."

"Waaaait!" Lisa shouted, racing back down the hall.

Slowly, Lauren stepped back and shut the door to her bedroom. She went to her desk, sat down, and began to write. But it was slow going. She kept stopping to listen to her siblings in the hall. The noise didn't bother her so much. What bothered her was that she couldn't join them.

When it was time for Lisa to go to bed, Lauren still hadn't finished her homework.

25

Retreating to the dining room table, she spread out her work and continued. How had she gotten so far behind? Why hadn't she taken more notes in class?

Because she hadn't been paying attention, that's why. She'd been letting her mind wander and not just to dreams of standing at center ice amid a shower of flowers, a gold medal around her neck. More and more often lately she had snapped to attention as the final bell rang to realize that a whole class had gone by and she couldn't remember what she'd been thinking about—or what the teacher had said.

Maybe that's why the homework seemed so much harder than usual. If you didn't listen in class, you had to put twice as much effort into homework.

It was like not giving your all in practice.

Lauren felt guilty—and the twinge of another, unfamiliar feeling. What was it?

Fear. She was, for the first time in her life, worried about doing well in school.

Setting her mouth in a tight line, Lauren bent over her books. She could do the work. She would do the work. And as long as her parents didn't find out about a few random low grades, everything would be just fine.

"You never called last night," Rebecca said.

She was waiting by Lauren's locker.

Lauren had been standing there, staring at her math test. Never in her life had she made such a low grade on a math test. Two points above failing the test. A D–. And a note from Mr. Santiago, her math teacher, saying, *See me after school today.*

"Lauren?"

The paper felt red-hot in Lauren's hand. Instinctively, she closed her fist around it, crumpling it into a ball and letting it drop to the bottom of the locker.

"What?" Lauren asked.

"Why didn't you call?"

"I started studying and when I stopped, it was too late," Lauren lied. The truth was, she'd forgotten. She'd forgotten until that very moment.

Why hadn't she told her the truth? Rebecca

would have understood, especially when she saw Lauren's math grade.

Or would she? Despite the fact that Lauren and Rebecca had been friends since first grade, they were very different. Numbers came so easily to Rebecca.

But Lauren and Rebecca had always been there for each other.

Until now. Now, with Lauren's schedule changed, and the extra work she was having to do just to try to keep up with her classes, Lauren had less and less time for her. She knew Rebecca had noticed it, knew Rebecca was trying to understand how important figure skating had become to her.

But Lauren knew that Rebecca really didn't understand. Lauren was worried about hurting Rebecca's feelings. Suddenly, she was worried about losing her best friend.

Just the thought of that happening made Lauren feel a little sick. Annie and Danielle were Lauren's best skating buddies, and they shared her love of the ice. But Rebecca was like family to Lauren. They'd swapped baby teeth and played together and picked each other first for games. In second grade they'd had a secret fort that they'd turned into their own museum full of natural wonders, like arrowheads and fossilized snail shells. In third grade, Lauren had stayed the whole weekend with Rebecca when Rebecca's favorite cat had died. She had helped bury the pet beneath the rose bush in the family's backyard. Rebecca knew that Lauren was secretly afraid of caterpillars, even the ones that eventually turned into butterflies.

Lauren said aloud again, "I'm sorry, Beck. It's really tough right now."

Rebecca made a face. "Tell me about it. I hate history. I can remember the dates, but I'm terrible with the names."

"When in doubt, say 'George Washington,'" suggested Lauren, slamming the locker door and leaving the disgraceful math test crumpled on the floor.

"But somehow, I don't think that George is the right answer to *every* question," Rebecca said. "I've got to get to class. Listen, meet me on the steps after school and we can walk home together. You don't go to the rink until four-thirty today, right?"

Trust Rebecca to remember her schedule when Lauren couldn't even remember to call her, Lauren thought guiltily. She hesitated. She'd meant to stay after school at the library today, but she couldn't tell Rebecca that without explaining what was going on.

"Okay," Lauren said.

"See ya," said Rebecca.

Not until she was gone did Lauren remember she was supposed to see her math teacher after class.

"Beck!" she called.

Rebecca turned.

"I might be a little late," Lauren said.

"Why?" Rebecca asked.

But Lauren pretended not to hear her as she turned and headed in the opposite direction.

4

"What took so long?" Rebecca was waiting on the front steps of Pine Creek Middle School as Lauren came out.

Lauren hesitated. Her conference with Mr. Santiago hadn't been so bad. He'd asked her if there was anything wrong that he could help her with and she had said that she just needed to study more. For a long moment, he'd weighed her answer, and Lauren had held her breath. What if he decided to call her parents? Or write them a note?

Then Mr. Santiago had nodded, pinching the bridge of his nose beneath his half glasses. "Okay, Lauren," he'd said. "But remember, if you need help, that's what teachers are for."

"Thanks," she'd gasped, trying not to sound too relieved.

The lie to Rebecca now came almost automatically. "I had to return a book to the school library before it was overdue."

"Oh," said Rebecca. They started down the steps. "So, how'd you do on your math test? You got that back today, didn't you?"

Once again, Rebecca's memory was perfect.

Lauren shrugged. "Yeah. It wasn't so bad. But I'll have to keep studying."

"I'll help if you want," offered Rebecca.

"Thanks," Lauren said. But right now, she didn't feel like telling Rebecca just how bad it was. She didn't want to admit it. She didn't really believe it herself. The situation was temporary, Lauren told herself. No reason to get everyone all upset. She could handle it.

It was only later that Lauren realized she'd begun to avoid her best friend. She came late to the class they had together so that they couldn't talk. She left lunch period early to go to the library to study. She pretended she had to get off the phone when Rebecca called.

As the days passed, Lauren realized the less she talked to Rebecca, the fewer lies she'd have to tell. The fewer lies she told, the less guilty she'd feel. And if she didn't feel so guilty, she'd have more energy to concentrate on keeping up with her schoolwork and her skating.

At least, that's what Lauren told herself.

To Lauren's relief, Rebecca didn't seem to notice. The days went by in a blur, and suddenly the only time of day Lauren looked forward to was her morning lessons with Coach Perry. On the ice, she thought only about making the next move perfect, worried only about remembering the order of the program on which she was working for the upcoming North Atlantic Regionals. For those who dreamed of being world-class skaters someday, the Regionals were the first step on the way.

And for Lauren, in her most secret dreams, the Regionals were the beginning, she hoped, of a trip to the Olympics. She wanted that more than anything in the world.

But she couldn't think about that now. Before she could go anywhere, she had to get her grades up and her life back in order. She was skating on thin ice. She'd ace her homework for math, only to get a low grade on her science homework. A good report for her language arts class meant that she somehow seemed to have a low grade on her math homework again. She was juggling everything faster and faster.

"Lauren?"

Lauren looked up from her book. "Hi, Beck."

"Aren't you going to come to lunch?"

"I already ate my sandwich," Lauren said. "I thought I'd do a little catch-up on my homework, so I got a library pass for lunch."

"What are you working on?" Rebecca asked.

"Just some math problems," Lauren said, sliding the paper under her book so Rebecca couldn't see it. She was redoing her math homework from the day before. It was one of Mr. Santiago's rules. He wouldn't accept a less than perfect math paper, so students who didn't get the answers right had to do their homework over.

Lately, Lauren had spent a lot of time doing her homework over for Mr. Santiago.

"You don't need any help in math, do you?" Rebecca said, sounding a little surprised.

"No," Lauren said. "It's just a homework redo for Mr. Santiago. You know how he is. I, ah, missed a problem." In fact, she'd missed half the problems, but Rebecca seemed satisfied with Lauren's explanation.

"I just wondered. I haven't talked to you in practically forever," Rebecca said.

Feeling like a rat, Lauren said, "We'll talk in Mrs. Campbell's class."

"Or maybe you could come over this afternoon after skating practice. We're fostering a mother cat with two kittens for the animal rescue shelter."

"Kittens?" For a moment, Lauren was tempted. She would love to go to Rebecca's house and do nothing but talk and laugh and play with the kittens. But she couldn't. "It'd be great, but I can't. Maybe next week, when my life isn't so crazy."

"I guess the new schedule is really hard," Rebecca said.

"It could be worse," Lauren said. To admit that she had reached a point where she couldn't handle everything on her own was too close to admitting failure. She couldn't do that. She forced herself to smile. "And it will be worse, if I don't get back to work."

"Well, okay," Rebecca said, not bothering to hide the disappointment in her voice. "See you later."

"Later," Lauren agreed, her eyes already refocusing on the page in front of her.

She got caught up in math. But she put off reading a story for language arts. She sat in horrified silence when Mrs. Campbell said cheerfully, "Pop quiz, students. Ten multiple choice questions."

For once, when Randy Bishop went into his throat-clutching, I'm-dying, total-panic routine, Lauren agreed with him. And for once, she didn't meet Rebecca's eyes to exchange a disgusted, can-you-believe-him? look.

Instead, she stared miserably down at the paper as Mrs. Campbell read out the questions about a story Lauren had not read.

On Friday when the tests were returned, Lauren stared in shock at her paper. "For every question you didn't get right," Mrs. Campbell announced, "I want a one-paragraph essay expanding on the correct answer for Monday. That means that those of you who got all ten answers right have no homework."

"Excellent," Rebecca said.

The bell rang, saving Lauren from telling Rebecca that she had failed the test. "I have to . . . to go to the bathroom," she gasped, and raced out of the room.

She splashed water on her face, a face that looked shocked and pale in the mirror. "It's just a little part of my grade," she told her reflection. "Anybody can fail a test. I can make it up."

But she'd never failed a test in her life. Panic engulfed her, blocking out everything else. She took a deep breath. And another. I'll do it this weekend, Lauren thought, starting in the school library right after my last class.

At the end of the day, moving at top speed, the words "Failure, failure, failure" drumming in her brain, Lauren threw open her locker and yanked out a notebook. The contents of the locker seemed to explode outward, crashing into her flailing arms and tumbling onto the floor before she could slam the locker door.

She stood numbly, feeling battered and tired. The perfect end to a perfectly awful day, she thought.

"Need some help?" Rebecca asked over Lauren's shoulder.

"No!" said Lauren, thinking for a moment that Rebecca was talking about Lauren's schoolwork. Then she realized Rebecca just meant help in clearing up the avalanche of books, notebooks, and papers that was spread out on the floor around her.

"You sure?" Rebecca asked in surprise.

"Ah, well, yeah. No problem. I've got it covered." What if Rebecca saw some of her homework papers with the low marks? Lauren couldn't risk that.

Trying to block Rebecca's view of the locker wreckage, she began to stuff books back inside.

"It's the weekend!" Rebecca said, her voice happy.

"Tell me about it." Lauren heard the deep gloom in her own voice, but she was too tired to care. She lifted the books and notebooks, trying to decide what to take home and what to leave at school. Was there even one subject she didn't have to work on this weekend?

"Mom's making double chocolate fudge cake tomorrow. With raspberry sauce," Rebecca went on.

"Mmmm," Lauren said. Realizing that Rebecca was waiting for her to say more, Lauren went on, "I'm going to spend my whole weekend studying and being stuck with costume pins. When I'm not practicing . . . but maybe I could come over Sunday to see the kittens."

"Sunday?" Rebecca said, an odd note in her voice.

"I'll call you," Lauren said, after a moment. She straightened. "Listen, I have to go by the library, so don't wait for me, okay?"

Rebecca blinked. "But . . ."

"Really. It's no problem. I'll talk to you later," Lauren said.

Drawing her books up in front of her like a shield, Rebecca took a step back. She stared at Lauren.

"Have a good weekend," Lauren said. "See ya."

She turned back to her locker.

"See you," Rebecca finally said, her voice flat. She turned and walked away.

Lauren immediately felt bad. I'll make it up to Rebecca, she thought. Once she had everything under control, she'd tell Rebecca about it, and they'd laugh and joke as they always did.

Lauren hoisted her backpack over her shoulder. As she staggered home, she tried to remember how happy she'd been when her life was more balanced between school and skating, family and friends. It would take a lot of work, but maybe, just maybe, she could get that balance back—before things spun out of control.

5

"Stand still," Mrs. Wing commanded.

"I *am* standing still," Lauren answered automatically.

"You're wiggling like a fish on a hook."

"Ugh," Lauren answered. "Yuck."

Her mother reached up and straightened Lauren's shoulders. "Raise your arms and hold them out," she told Lauren. "Good. Now don't move."

Lauren didn't move. It was the part she liked the least about having her skating costumes fitted.

I'm at center ice, she told herself. I've just finished a great program. I'm holding my pose while the crowd cheers. In a minute I'll wave and . . . but wait, my nose is itching.

Lauren wrinkled her nose. She blew upward, trying to make the itch go away. A strand of hair fell across her eyes. She scrunched her whole face.

Was one of her legs going to sleep? If she could just shift her weight a little bit . . .

"Lauren, be still," her mother warned.

"I am," Lauren said indignantly.

"Hah," said her mother. "Turn. A little more. Stop."

Her nose was still itching. She wanted to sneeze. Her leg was definitely going to sleep. In a minute, she might topple over, when it went completely numb. She'd be stuck full of pins. She might break something, like her arm or her other leg.

Cautiously, she flexed the muscles of her leg.

"Be still," her mother said again.

"How much longer?" Lauren asked.

"Not much longer—if you don't move." Her mother kept pinning and poking and humming. Finally, finally, Mrs. Wing said, "That's it."

In a whirlwind of motion, Lauren scratched

her nose, brushed the hair off her face, and shook out her sleeping leg, hopping around from one foot to the other. "Whew," she said.

"We're making progress," her mother said with satisfaction. "Take a look."

Turning, Lauren faced herself in the full-length mirror on the back of her parents' bedroom door. Her white socks were scrunched at her ankles. She had on the WNBA basketball cap that her brother had given her. And she was wearing the costume for the short program that her mother was making, or part of the costume. She'd chosen daffodil yellow, to go with the quick movements, soaring jumps, and athletic choreography of the piece. The material that made up the body of the costume had a satiny sheen. The sheer sleeves hadn't been fitted to the costume yet, so Lauren's bare arms stuck out. And yards and yards of the delicate swirling lace that her mother had basted to a lace sash at Lauren's waist hung limply around Lauren's knees.

Lauren made a face in the mirror. "This is progress?" she asked.

Her mother made a face back. "Consider it

the 'before' picture. Like those before and after photographs in the magazines, when they give people makeovers."

"Yeah, except sometimes the after pictures are worse than the before ones," Lauren said.

"Oh, you!" Mrs. Wing gave Lauren a light swat on the leg. "Get off the stool and get out of the costume so I can get to work. And so you can wiggle as much as you want."

"Gee, thanks," said Lauren. She hopped off the stool and peeled out of the costume in record time, resuming her jeans and sweatshirt gratefully.

Mrs. Wing looked at her watch. "Or we could go shopping. We've got about an hour before we need to start dinner."

"No, thanks," Lauren said. "It's not my favorite sport, especially on Saturday."

"Fine by me." Mrs. Wing began to gather up the stray straight pins that had escaped while she was fitting the costume to Lauren. "But I thought you said you needed to get Rebecca a birthday present."

Lauren froze. "Oh no! Today's Rebecca's birthday," she croaked.

And she remembered Rebecca saying in the hall the day before, *Mom's making double chocolate fudge cake. With raspberry sauce.* It was Rebecca's favorite cake and she always had it for her birthday.

Then she heard her own voice saying, *Have a good weekend. I'll call you.*

How could she have been so forgetful? So stupid?

How could Rebecca ever forgive her?

"Lauren?" her mother said.

"I'll be right back," Lauren gasped. "Don't go anywhere." And before her mother could answer, Lauren had dashed out of the room.

Hardly knowing what she was doing, she punched in Rebecca's number and waited. One ring. Two rings. Three.

"Hello?"

"Rebecca! Happy birthday!" Lauren said.

Silence. Then Rebecca said in a flat voice, "Thanks."

"Is the cake ready yet? Does your house smell like a chocolate factory? Are you . . ."

"You forgot my birthday," Rebecca said.

"Until just now. Didn't you?" Surprisingly, her voice didn't sound accusing. It only sounded interested, as if she were in science class and asking about the results of an experiment.

"No! I mean, not really . . ."

"Yes, you did," Rebecca cut her off. "At first, I thought maybe it was going to be a surprise party and you were just pretending you forgot. But then I realized that you just didn't remember at all."

"Rebecca!"

Lauren heard voices in the background. "Please hold on for a minute," Rebecca said.

At least she hadn't hung up, Lauren thought. She gripped the phone so tightly, her knuckles grew pale. Then Lauren heard Rebecca say, "I'll be right there, Mom."

When Rebecca got back on the line, Lauren said, "Beck. Rebecca. Listen, I'm really sorry. I didn't mean to forget. It's just that everything has been so crazy . . ."

Once again, Rebecca cut Lauren off. "You forgot my birthday."

"Only for a little while. Temporary insanity,

that's all," Lauren said weakly.

"Thanks for calling," Rebecca said. "I have to go."

"Beck, wait!"

But Rebecca had hung up the phone.

"Lauren?" Her mother came down the stairs. "Is everything okay?"

"Ah. . . . Yes," Lauren lied. "But you're right, Mom. I do need to go shopping for Rebecca's birthday gift. Thanks for reminding me."

"Hurry up, then," her mother said. "You've got five minutes to get ready."

Lauren took the stairs two at a time. She was about to clean out her piggy bank to buy Rebecca an extra-special birthday gift. The new skating boots Lauren had been saving for would have to wait a little longer. This was an emergency. Lauren knew just what to buy: a silver bracelet made of cats, each cat chasing the tail of the cat in front of it, silver paws curled around silver tails. Lauren had been with Rebecca at the mall when she had admired it.

Soon Lauren and her mom were at the mall, having the clerk wrap that very bracelet. Would it help soothe her best friend's hurt feelings? Lauren hoped so. She counted out the money, with the fear that not all the money in the universe would make Rebecca forgive Lauren and understand.

For the rest of the weekend, Lauren kept the box, wrapped in silver paper with a red-and-silver-striped ribbon, on her desk. She kept calling Rebecca. But Rebecca didn't return Lauren's phone calls. Lauren turned the pages of her books, feeling scared and somehow lost.

Rebecca's steps slowed she as approached her locker Monday morning. Lauren had been there since the doors of the school had opened, leaning against her best friend's locker.

Now Lauren straightened and smiled. Her lips felt tight.

"Hi," she said. Her voice sounded funny.

"What are you doing here?" Rebecca asked, in a voice that had no expression at all.

"Waiting for you," Lauren said. "Beck, I . . . it was really stupid of me . . . I wish that . . ."

All the speeches Lauren had practiced in her

head skittered away before Rebecca's unblinking stare. At last Lauren gave up. She thrust the box at Rebecca. "Happy birthday, a little late," she said. "Please forgive me, Beck."

For a moment, Lauren saw Rebecca's face soften. Then her lips tightened. "I don't want a present," Rebecca said. "You think a present can make up for you forgetting my birthday?"

"No . . . but . . . well, it's a really nice present," Lauren said. She regretted the words the moment they were out of her mouth.

Rebecca's eyes blazed with sudden, uncharacteristic anger. "A really *nice* present? You think you can buy me? Spend lots of money on some stupid birthday gift and that will make everything all right?"

"No, of course not! I just wanted to get you something extra-special to say I'm sorry and happy birthday. Beck, please."

Lauren shoved the small box into Rebecca's hand. Rebecca's fingers closed over it automatically.

Then, half afraid that Rebecca might throw the box back at her, Lauren turned and fled.

Lauren didn't see Rebecca again until Mrs. Campbell's language arts class.

When Rebecca sat down next to Lauren in her usual seat, Lauren's hopes rose. She looked at Rebecca's wrist. But no silver bracelet glinted there.

Rebecca turned and met Lauren's eyes. "Thank you for my present," she said. "The bracelet is very pretty." She sounded a lot like Lisa saying thank you for a birthday gift she didn't particularly like—after being prompted by her mother.

Then Rebecca turned and faced the front of the room. She didn't speak to Lauren or meet her eyes for the rest of the class.

"You *forgot* Rebecca's birthday? Fifteen toe loops and a back flip!" exclaimed Annie, stopping short just as she was about to step off the ice.

Danielle staggered back, clutching the railing of the rink. "You *didn't*," she said. "That is totally the absolute worst! How could you?"

"Thanks for making me feel better," Lauren said.

"Have you apologized?" Annie asked.

"Told her you were sorry, sorry, sorry, and you'd rather be skates-up dead than do something like forget her birthday?" Danielle added.

"Yes," Lauren said. "At least I tried to. But she didn't exactly give me the chance." She gave Annie a little push. "Hey, move it. I don't want to stand on the ice all day."

Remembering where she was, Annie stepped out of the rink and sat down to slip on her blade guards. Lauren and Danielle did the same and they headed for the locker rooms.

"She kept the birthday present I gave her," Lauren said. "A bracelet."

"Good," said Annie.

"But she hasn't worn it yet."

"Bad," said Danielle.

"Give her time," Annie said. "She'll come around. I get angry, but I never stay angry long."

"But you have lots of practice at getting over it. You have a, well, a bad temper," Lauren said.

"Gee, thanks," said Annie.

"You know what I mean," said Lauren.

Annie rolled her eyes. "Yeah, I do. But I prefer to think of it as a quick temper, not a bad one."

"Whatever," Lauren said.

They changed into their regular clothes and headed for the entrance to the rink.

"My costume is ready for the competition. At last," Danielle announced, changing the topic to one of her favorite subjects. "Wait till you see it."

Accepting the sudden turn the conversation had taken, Lauren said, "You're lucky. My mom spent half of Saturday sticking pins in my costume. And in me."

"Wouldn't it be nice if you could just punch a button on a computer and your costume would appear?" Annie said.

Computers, thought Lauren with a pang. Had Rebecca gotten a computer for her birthday, as she'd hoped? Lauren hadn't even asked her.

She let her thoughts wander as Annie and Danielle talked about the upcoming competition and about costumes until they were on the steps outside the entrance to the rink. Then Annie punched Lauren lightly on the shoulder. "Good luck," she said. "It'll be okay."

"In about a thousand years," Danielle blurted out.

"Danielle!" Annie gave Danielle an annoyed look.

"Sorry," Danielle said. "I just meant, it's going to take time."

"So all I have to do is wait," Lauren said.

"Something like that," Danielle agreed.

A horn sounded. "See you tomorrow," Annie said, bounding down the steps.

"Later," said Danielle, as her family's car pulled up behind Annie's.

"Right," said Lauren. She waved and headed for her bicycle. How long would she have to wait before Rebecca forgave her?

Then she got on her bike and pedaled home, thinking about how she might have lost her best friend forever with every turn of the wheel.

She tried to look on the bright side. Not everything in her life was a mess. She'd managed to stay on top of her social studies and language arts work. But Lauren couldn't shake the uneasy feeling that her parents might not feel as optimistic.

6

The silence was worse than anything her parents could say.

Lauren clasped her hands in front of her and stared down at her interlaced fingers.

Dinner was over. Somewhere upstairs, Bryan was doing homework. Lacey was helping Lisa get ready for bed. Lacey and Bryan had had good report cards. Lisa, who was in kindergarten, was too young to have a report card.

Lauren's mother had opened Lauren's report card and then, after a long moment, pushed it across to Lauren's father. It lay there now. Lauren could read it upside down, but she didn't need to see it. She knew what it said.

It was the worst report card she had ever had. All her work had raised her grade in social studies and math to a B– and a C+. But she should have had an A– and a B in these subjects. Her A– in language arts was one bright spot. But somehow, in all the studying she had done, she had let science, her worst subject, slide into the basement. She'd made a D.

Her father said gently, "Lauren, honey, how did this happen? You're usually such a good student, and you've always liked school."

"I'm not sure," Lauren said. She almost wished they would yell or be angry. This gentle puzzlement was much worse. "And I *do* like school," Lauren added. "I know this doesn't show it."

"You studied every morning, going to and from the Silver Springs rink," Mr. Wing went on. "I saw you."

"I know," Lauren said miserably.

"Is it too much, this new schedule you're on?" asked her mother. Her face was concerned, her forehead wrinkled in a worried frown.

"No!" Lauren exclaimed. "Oh, no!"

"Then how do you explain this?" Her mother indicated the report card. "I know science has never been your favorite subject, but you've never gotten a D in your life."

"I know," Lauren said. She squeezed her hands together. She could feel tears gathering in the corners of her eyes.

"You must have known your grades were going down," her father said. "I don't think this report card is a surprise to you."

Lauren shook her head, trying not to cry. She wasn't crying about her grades so much as about everything. Rebecca would still barely speak to her. She had worked harder than she had ever worked in her life on her schoolwork. But it still hadn't been enough. And now she'd disappointed her parents. Everything was out of control, off balance. And Lauren couldn't understand why.

She only knew that she felt awful.

"Lauren," her mother said and put her hand out to cover Lauren's clenched fingers.

Lauren swallowed the tears and looked up. "Yes?"

"What happened?" her mother said.

"I don't know," Lauren wailed. And then she told them everything from the first bad grade to the awful moment when she realized that she had forgotten Rebecca's birthday.

"And now Rebecca's still mad at me, and I've flunked science," Lauren finished.

"You didn't flunk," her father said. He was a stickler for accuracy.

With a trembling smile, Lauren said, "I might as well have."

"It *has* been too much for you," her mother said. "Lessons in the mornings, practices every afternoon."

"NO! No, it hasn't. Please, *please* don't make me stop taking lessons from Coach Perry," Lauren said. "Please!"

She'd expected her parents to tell her they'd think it over. She'd expected them to tell her that they'd discuss her bad grades and decide what to do. She half-expected them to ground her from everything, right then and there.

But they didn't.

Her father took a pen from his pocket and

signed the bottom of the report card. He handed it back to Lauren.

"You're . . . are you going to ground me . . . am I . . . how much trouble am I in?" Lauren stammered.

Her mother stood up and came around to lay her cheek against Lauren's head, briefly. Then she straightened. "Oh, Lauren. We're not going to punish you. In fact, I think you've punished yourself enough these past few weeks. It sounds as if you've been pretty unhappy."

"It's been awful," Lauren admitted.

Leaning back in his chair, Lauren's father said, "I think this has been too much, too fast."

Lauren's heart sank.

"Let's think this over and decide how we can make it possible for you to continue skating and continue to do well in school," he went on.

Mrs. Wing sat down beside Lauren. She tapped the report card with one finger. "What subjects do you need the most help in—besides science?"

Lauren stared down at the row of numbers. "I've brought my grades up in everything. And

I'm pretty sure that by next grading period, I'll make As and Bs again . . . except science. I mean, I'm going to have to work twice as hard at that and I'm not very good at it."

"Maybe a tutor would help," suggested Mr. Wing.

"I could ask Ms. Ivens for some help," Lauren said reluctantly. She didn't want to do that. Ms. Ivens clearly loved the subject she taught, but Ms. Ivens had little patience with students who didn't quickly pick up what she taught, or love science the way she did.

"Will you talk to her about this?" Mrs. Wing asked. "Or do you want me to?"

"I will," said Lauren. "I should have talked to her before now."

Her mother nodded almost absently. Her eyes were narrowed and she had a distant expression on her face. Then she looked over at Lauren's father. He raised his eyebrows.

They were having one of those silent parent conversations that Lauren could never decode. Eyebrow language, she called it.

Her mother turned her attention back to

WINNING MOMENTS

Michelle Kwan won the Gold Medal at the 2000 U.S. Figure Skating Championships in Cleveland, Ohio.

Skating Dreams #2: Staying Balanced

Skating Dreams is published by Hyperion Paperbacks for Children. All rights reserved.

Photo © 2000 by David Black

Lauren. "I also think that, at least for the time being, you are going to have to cut back on your practice time at Pine Creek rink in the afternoons."

"But . . ."

Mrs. Wing held up her hand. "You can go once a week, on a day you don't have a skating lesson. And you can practice on the weekends as usual. But I think it would be best if you concentrated on catching up solidly in every subject, as well as bringing your grade up in science."

"The Regionals are coming," Lauren said. "What if that's not enough practice? What if . . ."

"Next grading period, we'll review the situation and make adjustments accordingly," her father said. "I think that's fair, don't you?"

She had to admit, deep down, that her parents were being fair—as much as she disliked the thought of cutting back on skating even the tiniest bit. I'm lucky they are still letting me take the lessons, she told herself. She forced herself to nod. "Yes," she answered her father's question. "I guess so."

She'd just have to make every moment on the ice count double. She took a deep breath. "Can I go to the rink tomorrow afternoon and tell Annie and Danielle?"

"Yes, of course," her mother said. "But come home afterward, okay? No practice this week. One afternoon practice per week from now on, until those grades come up."

Lauren stood up, forcing a smile. "Well," she said. "I guess I'd better get started on my homework."

Outside, she was smiling. But inside, she felt sad and lonely and very, very tired.

7

"Only once a week? Double-*death* spiral," gasped Annie.

Danielle peered into Lauren's face. "You're being very brave. I'd be crying so hard, I would be blinded with tears. Still weeping as I walked away from the skating rink . . ."

"I already cried," Lauren said, cutting Danielle off.

Danielle didn't mind. She was used to people's failure to appreciate her dramatic talents. "I know," she said. She patted Lauren's arm.

"So you're not even practicing with us today?" Annie asked.

Lauren shook her head. "I'll be here next

Tuesday. I can practice in the afternoon once a week, on the day I don't have a skating lesson in the morning. That's Tuesday."

"This is terrible," Danielle cried. "But it's not forever." Even though it'll feel like it, Lauren added silently.

"What now?" Annie asked.

"I get a tutor in science." Lauren made a face. That was one agony she'd been spared that day: Ms. Ivens had been out sick with the flu. The substitute had turned the class into a study hall so Lauren had spent her science period reading and underlining her science book.

As long as Ms. Ivens was out sick, Lauren wouldn't have to talk to her about tutoring.

"And then?" Annie prompted.

"And then I raise all my grades and at the end of the grading period, I get to start skating more again."

"And maybe Rebecca starts speaking to you again," Danielle said. "Maybe she feels *sooo* sorry for you, seeing you suffering in pain and misery that she forgives you."

Lauren felt a little stab of real, extra misery

in her chest. "Maybe," she said.

"At least you weren't forced to give up your skating lessons," Annie said tactfully, changing the subject back to one a little less painful.

"At least," agreed Lauren.

Annie looked past Lauren, and said in a loud voice, "Well, Lauren, good luck at the dentist. See you later."

"What?" said Lauren.

"Later," added Danielle, and her two friends skated quickly away. Lauren turned to see Erica clomping toward her.

Oh, great, Lauren thought with an inward groan. She turned it into a moan of agony worthy of Danielle, clapped one hand to her face, gasped, "My tooth, my tooth," and hurried past Erica.

Startled, Erica gave way, and for once Lauren managed to leave the skating rink and Erica's vicinity without any close encounters of the mean and nasty kind.

So the day wasn't a total loss after all.

Thunk, thunk, swish, thunkthunk.
Thunk, thunk, swish, thunkthunk.

Subtract two, divide by—

THUNK, slam, rattle, thunkthunk.

Lauren put down her pencil. Her math homework kept getting mixed up with the game of basketball her brother was playing outside the garage.

With a yawn, Lauren looked at her watch. Ten minutes until time to help with dinner. She might as well take a break now.

She slid out of her chair and went down to visit her brother.

"Hey, Wing," Bryan greeted her.

"Hey, Wing," Lauren returned.

Her brother fired the ball at her. She posted up and put it in.

"Not bad," he said.

She passed the ball to him and he spun and tried to do an over-the-shoulder slam dunk. The only thing he slammed was his body against the garage door. The ball hit the basket, bounced up and then onto the garage roof. It rolled slowly down to the gutter, then began to travel along it to the corner of the garage.

Lauren went to catch the ball as it came down.

66

It didn't. It stayed lodged on the corner of the gutter.

Bryan came to stand beside her. They stared up at the ball. Then Bryan executed a couple of monster jumps. But they weren't monster enough. He couldn't quite reach the ball.

"Swing up," he said and lifted Lauren to his shoulder. She stretched upward. "Gutter needs cleaning," she reported.

"And I know who'll get to do it," Bryan said. "Right now, let's concentrate on basketball."

Lauren grabbed the ball and slid off her brother's shoulder.

"Teamwork," Bryan said. "Wonderful, isn't it? Now pass me the ball. I want to try that shot again."

Lauren bounced the ball thoughtfully. Her brother was always talking about teamwork. "No teamwork, no win," he said, quoting his coach.

"Bryan," she said.

"That's me. That's a basketball," he said. "Pass the basketball to brother Bryan."

She palmed the ball, making big, slow, fat

bounces. "Do you like everybody on your team? Your hockey team?"

"What other team is there? And no, I don't," said Bryan. "The basketball?"

"But you play with them," Lauren persisted. "Even if you don't like them."

"Hey, you can't do everything yourself. And it's a lot easier to get the job done if you're working with people you at least try to get along with."

"But . . ."

"They're my teammates. Even the ones who are jerks, as long as they do their job on the ice and don't do totally disgusting things off the ice, then I'm going to get along with them."

Lauren thought about this, and bounced the ball some more.

Bryan gave up and folded his arms. "Not like figure skating, I guess," he said. "I mean, you're on your own out there." He shook his head at the awfulness of it.

"Not all my teammates are jerks," Bryan added. "After a few practices, we started to bond, you know. I discovered they weren't so bad after all." Her brother's grin widened. "And if they had something to teach me, something they were sharper at than me . . . well, we started hanging out more and became friends."

Lauren stared at her brother. An idea was beginning to form in her mind, an idea so obvious that she couldn't believe she hadn't thought of it immediately.

"Bryan," she said. "You're a genius. Brilliant. The Mount Everest of Brains."

"Yeah? Then throw me the ball."

Lauren threw the ball to her brother. He grabbed it, faked left, faked right, pivoted, and shouted, "He shoots, he . . ."

The ball went up on the roof, bounced once, and came back down—through the basket.

". . . scores," Bryan said. "I meant to do that. Really, I did."

Laughing, feeling more hopeful than she had in a long time, Lauren went into the house.

8

"Just a moment, Lauren. . . ."

"Wait! Please. Would you tell her it's about schoolwork?" Lauren asked.

Mrs. Meyers said, "You know, I hope you two work this out soon. I hate being the answering machine."

"I'm sorry, Mrs. Meyers."

"Don't be sorry, Lauren. I'll march Rebecca to the phone, but I'm not guaranteeing quality conversation."

"Thanks." Lauren missed Rebecca. And she missed Rebecca's family, too, especially Rebecca's unconventional mother. And their seven cats and two dachshunds. And . . .

Someone picked up the phone. After a long moment, Rebecca said, "Hello."

Without realizing it, Lauren let out a long sigh of relief. "Beck," she said, "I need your help."

Another long moment passed. Then Rebecca said, "What kind of help?"

"School. I . . . I made D in science."

"A *D!*" The careful calmness left Rebecca's voice. It must have gone up an octave. "*You* made a *D*?"

"Yes. And I'm having to give up all but one of my afternoon practices a week until my grades go back up. And if they don't go up . . ." Lauren let the possibilities of that hang in the air and then was almost sorry she had. Imagining what would happen if she couldn't raise her grades was worse than saying it aloud.

"Are your parents going to stop you from skating?" Rebecca asked.

"No." Lauren paused, a dramatic pause worthy of Danielle. "Not yet. But I have to get a tutor. And I don't want to ask Ms. Ivens."

"Ms. Ivens," Rebecca repeated, almost to herself. "No. I can see that."

"So I wondered if you would tutor me. In science. And maybe help out in a few other things if it gets bad. But mainly science. Just for a little while," Lauren rushed on.

This time the pause was so long that Lauren said, "Rebecca?"

"I'm still here. I have to think about it. I'll let you know."

"When? I really, really need your help," Lauren said. "I can't do it without you."

It was melodrama Danielle-style. But it was also true, Lauren realized. She didn't think she could get out of this total life slump without Rebecca's help—not just her tutoring, but her friendship and support.

"I'll let you know tomorrow. I'll meet you outside the school office," Rebecca said.

"Thanks," said Lauren. "Thanks, Rebecca."

"I haven't said I would do it," Rebecca said. "Good-bye."

Lauren put the phone down. Then she did a little dance in the middle of the family room.

"You haven't said you wouldn't, either," she said, and thought of Bryan's words—*If they had something to teach me . . . well we started hanging out more and became friends.*

"Is that skating?" Lisa asked. Lauren looked up to see her youngest sister standing in the doorway.

"You bet," Lauren said. "Totally happy, flying on ice skating. The very best kind."

"This morning," Coach Perry said, "you are a frog."

"A frog?" Lauren repeated, startled. She tucked her mittened hands under her arms and stood in front of her coach, breathing heavily.

"A graceful frog," Coach Perry said, with one of her quick smiles. "You leap with energy, you spring across the ice. Your short program is in good shape."

"It's what I do best," said Lauren. She wasn't being conceited. It was true. The athletic leaps and energetic swoops of the short program that Coach Perry and Lauren had planned came easily to Lauren, especially today. She couldn't tell Coach Perry, but her conversation with Rebecca had made her feel hopeful and happy and had given her extra energy.

"This is true," Coach Perry said. "And you practice it more on your own, I believe."

How did Coach Perry know that? Lauren nodded sheepishly.

"It's natural to like to practice what you are good at, what is easy. Many good skaters do this. Great skaters practice the hard parts. So now we will practice what does not come so easily."

Coach Perry was referring to the long program. The grace and artistry that the gently soaring music of the long program required was more difficult for Lauren. Morning after morning, she found herself trying to stretch her arms out to what seemed impossible lengths, to curve her leg just so, while pointing her toe at the exact angle that her coach demanded.

This morning was no different, except for one thing. Lauren's mood had lightened, and it lent a certain lightness even to the moves that still felt clumsy. At the end of the practice, she felt worthy of Coach Perry's nod of approval.

"I'll practice the long program," she promised as she left.

"I thought you would," said Coach Perry enigmatically, before turning to head for her office.

But first, Lauren thought, walking toward her locker, I have to get to school, and start practicing being a good friend again—if Rebecca will let me.

Rebecca was waiting for Lauren as she came out of the school office. Lauren studied Rebecca's face as Rebecca approached. Her straight dark eyebrows weren't frowning. But her brown eyes were serious, her gaze was steady. Was this good or bad?

"Hi," Lauren said, trying to sound cheerful and friendly and not too sure that Rebecca would give her another chance.

"Hi," said Rebecca. She shifted her red messenger bag. "I can give you two afternoons a week, right after school. I think we should meet in the school library. Fewer distractions and it will be easier to concentrate. Are Wednesday and Friday okay with you for this week? We can change the days around if you have a test."

"Wednesday and Friday are fine," Lauren said. An enormous surge of relief washed over.

"Good," said Rebecca. "I'll see you Wednesday afternoon."

She hitched up her messenger bag and joined the stream of students flowing down the hall.

"Thanks," Lauren said. But Rebecca had already gone.

It's a start, Lauren thought. I think. At least she has to talk to me, two afternoons a week. No way she can tutor me without doing that.

But she knew that Rebecca wasn't ready to forgive her yet. Lauren had a lot of hard work ahead of her, in every way.

9

"Think of science as an art, like figure skating," Rebecca said. Her voice was patient. "When you do an experiment, you are recording patterns, just like the patterns you make on the ice. Only you're not making the patterns. You're like the referee or judge. You're observing the patterns and writing them down."

"Right," said Lauren. "Patterns."

"So we'll do this next problem, and we'll write it down, and then we'll compare what we figured out from the patterns," Rebecca said.

"Okay," said Lauren meekly. She stared down at her book. It was Friday, and Rebecca was being a stern taskmaster. She didn't joke, and she hadn't softened up, as Lauren had hoped she would. On the other hand, she was a natural teacher. She found ways of explaining things that made it easier for Lauren to understand.

The school library was quiet. They were the only students left. On Friday afternoons, Pine Creek Middle School emptied quickly.

If they'd been at Lauren's house, or Rebecca's, they could have taken a break for sodas. And if they'd taken a break, they might have been able to talk. Lauren knew better than to try to bring up how she had forgotten her best friend's birthday, but she thought if they could just make ordinary conversation, Rebecca might loosen up. And from there, they might slip back into the old habits and patterns of friendship, at least a little.

"Let's take a break," Lauren suggested, when they'd finished the next problem.

Rebecca glanced at her watch. "Okay. Five minutes."

"I'm going to get a drink of water," Lauren said. "Want to come?"

"No, thanks," said Rebecca. "I'll just work on my own homework."

She pulled her notebook toward her, dismissing Lauren.

Lauren sighed inwardly, but she said cheerfully, "Okay. See you in five."

Rebecca's always been stubborn, she reminded herself, as she bent over the water fountain. She straightened, smiling. After all, it's one of the things I like about her.

When they'd finished for the day, Rebecca walked out of the school with Lauren. On the front stairs she said, "How's everything going? The skating, I mean."

She wasn't looking at Lauren. She was staring out at the scramble of kids on the soccer fields.

"It's hard not being able to practice every afternoon," Lauren said. "I know it's only been a week, but I miss being at the rink. And I'm afraid I'll lose my edge. The Regionals are coming up, you know."

Rebecca nodded. She'd heard Lauren talk about the Regionals often. "If your grades get better, you can go back to practicing in the afternoons, right?"

"Right," said Lauren. "Not that I don't *love* science . . ."

Amazingly, Rebecca actually smiled. "I know you do," she said. "Don't worry about your science grade. I'll have you back on the ice in the shortest amount of time scientifically and mathematically possible."

"I'm counting on it," said Lauren.

"You can," said Rebecca. "See you Monday." She went down the steps. Lauren stayed where she was a minute longer, smiling herself. It might not be in the shortest amount of time scientifically and mathematically possible, but maybe she would have her best friend back soon, too.

"It was like, the worst movie in the entire movie world," Annie said. In the background, Lauren heard laughter and gagging sounds. "Moira left and went to get a soda, but Danielle and I stayed so we could laugh at all the lame scary parts."

"It sounds like fun," Lauren said.

"Hi, Lauren!" Danielle called.

"Danielle has *no* phone manners," Annie said. "And guess who was there?"

"Who?"

"Randy. From your class, right? He was being a complete nerd."

"That's Randy, then," Lauren said.

"He was pretty funny," Danielle said loudly.

"Puh-lease," Lauren said. "I bet I can guess what he was doing. Was he standing on his seat, taking bows?"

"Well, he did that, too, until the usher came and made him stop," Annie said. "He also tried to balance a bucket of popcorn on his nose. Total disaster."

It was Saturday night. Annie's older sister Moira had taken Annie and Danielle to the movies and then for a sleepover at Annie's house. They'd invited Lauren, but Lauren had decided not to join them. She knew she wasn't exactly grounded, but she didn't want to push her luck with her parents. It was safer, and probably wiser, to stay home and concentrate on her homework.

"Anyway, we missed you. Next time, you have to come," Annie concluded.

"Next time, I will," Lauren promised. She hung up the phone and stared down at the book she was reading. She was going to do a book report in language arts for extra credit. She'd chosen a book called *Dogsong*, about sled dogs. Mrs. Campbell had mentioned the author often, and Lauren could tell he was one of her favorites.

Of course, I'd probably like any book with ice in it, thought Lauren wryly. It helped that this story was set in a land of ice.

For a moment she felt a pang of loneliness, as if she were all alone out in the snow, as lost as, well, a lost dog. Stop being silly, Lauren scolded herself. I may not be spending the night at Annie's, but it's not as if my friends have all abandoned me.

So what if they were having fun while she was working? It wasn't the end of the world.

Reaching over, she scooped her cat, Lutz, from his place on the bed. He protested but allowed her to settle him onto her lap. Feeling him purr, Lauren felt a little less lonely.

She wrenched her thoughts away from her friends at play, and focused again on her book and the frozen world where the story was set, petting Lutz absently as she read.

Maybe I could do a science report on ice, she thought. I could call it "From Icebergs to Ice Cubes." She made a face, and began to read.

10

The girl in the mirror extended her arms. She bent her knees and slid forward, spun on one foot, and landed.

The girl in the mirror made a face and cried, "Ouch!" and bounced out of sight, hopping on one foot.

Like a one-legged kangaroo, Lauren hopped around the cramped bedroom, folding herself up at last into the chair at her desk. She glared at the curved foot of the heavy, battered old chest of drawers.

It was that curve that had met her foot as she'd practiced the moves of her short program. The wooden foot had won.

She rubbed her toes. The room was too small to really practice, but she'd wanted to watch herself in the mirror and make sure she wasn't practicing any bad habits, like holding her arms unevenly.

Lauren sighed. She looked at the mirror. She looked out the window. It was still early and she'd done all the homework she could stand to do before dinner. Her parents hadn't said she couldn't practice at all, they'd just said she couldn't go to the rink.

Tipping her head back, she thought about this. Then she bounded to her feet, dug her old high-tops out of the back of the closet, and laced them on. Carefully, she unhooked the mirror from the door and carried it down the stairs. The house was quiet. Her brother was still at school, Lacey was at a friend's house, and Lisa was at the restaurant with her parents.

Lauren took the mirror out into the backyard and propped it against one side of Lisa's swing set.

Then she walked out onto the grass, raised her arms and her chin, and imagined that she was not in her own backyard but at center ice.

She went through all the moves of her long program as best she could, concentrating on making long, smooth lines with her arms and legs and her body. Then she did it again, and then again.

Her shadow grew longer as she practiced, but she lost track of time.

When the back door banged open, she jumped.

"Lauren?"

"Mom! Hi," Lauren said. She lowered her arms.

"I've been calling you," her mother said.

"Sorry. I didn't even know you were home," Lauren said.

Mrs. Wing raised one eyebrow. "So I see." She looked at the mirror and then at Lauren.

"I finished most of my homework," Lauren said. "We didn't have much today, so I thought I'd . . ." Her voice trailed off and she gestured toward the mirror.

Her mother studied her for a moment longer. Then she said, "Well, be careful when you put the mirror back. And don't forget to wash your hands before dinner."

"Okay," said Lauren. She raised her arms again, and met her own eyes in the mirror. She tried to see herself as one of the judges might see her, or someone in the audience. She imagined herself not in jeans and a sweatshirt and scruffy high-top sneakers, but in the beautiful new skating costume her mother was just finishing.

"'From Icebergs to Ice Cubes'?" Rebecca repeated. "You're kidding, right?" She and Lauren were in the library. It was another Friday afternoon.

"Well, I have to do a science report that's going to be one-fourth of my grade this grading period, so I figure I should do it on something I'm sort of familiar with," Lauren said.

"Ice," said Rebecca.

"Ice," agreed Lauren. "I mean, after all, where do I spend most of my time?"

"School," Rebecca said. "Sleeping."

"Okay, okay, then where would I *like* to spend most of my time?"

"Skating," Rebecca conceded. She looked at Lauren. "If you could skate all day long, instead of go to school, would you?"

"Yes," said Lauren, without hesitation.

A small frown creased the bridge of Rebecca's nose as she considered this. "And I guess you'd spend any free time you had left over skating, too?"

"No." Lauren gave Rebecca an impish look. "I'd spend some of that time taking my friends with me to watch figure skating competitions— with a time-out now and then for ice cream."

"Do you miss it?" Rebecca asked, with unexpected seriousness.

Lauren didn't have to ask Rebecca what she meant. "Yes," she said. "But I've been practicing at home. In the backyard. And I go over my routines for the long and short programs every night in my head until I go to sleep."

"Wow," said Rebecca, almost to herself.

"I guess it's kind of weird, isn't it," Lauren said.

"N-no," said Rebecca. "Not weird. Dedicated. Intensely dedicated." She paused.

"Like it means more to you than anything else in the world."

"Well, yeah," said Lauren, trying to keep it light. "Sort of like that."

"I don't know," said Rebecca. "I guess I've never felt that way about anything. I mean, except my family."

"There are other important things in life, just as important," Lauren said. "Family. Friends."

Rebecca didn't acknowledge this. Instead, she said briskly, "Okay. Out of the backyard and onto the ice. From icebergs to ice cubes, no. Now that *is* weird, too weird, especially for Ms. Ivens."

"I thought it might be," Lauren said in a meek voice.

"But you could do something on global warming," Rebecca said. "The effect of it on the Arctic and Antarctica. You know, what happens when all that ice starts to melt."

"We build big freezers?" Lauren said.

Rebecca rolled her eyes. "Stick to ice skating," she said. "And I'll stick to science. Let's get to work."

That weekend, Lauren learned more about ice, icebergs, and global warming than she thought possible. When Rebecca suggested they meet at the Pine Creek library, Lauren gladly agreed. At the end of the afternoon, Lauren had acquired a notebook full of information. It was fun to do research, and it felt great to be spending time with Rebecca again.

"If you want," Rebecca said, "We could spend a little time on my new computer and see if we can add to this. Maybe download some graphics."

"That would be good," Lauren said. Inside, she was shouting with joy.

"Okay," said Rebecca.

Lauren was so happy to go to Rebecca's house. Mr. Meyers smiled as he opened the door. "Lauren," he said. "We haven't seen you for a while, have we?"

"No," said Lauren.

"Well, I'm glad to see you again. Been keeping yourself busy?"

"Pretty busy," said Lauren, following him

into the house and making her way to Rebecca's room.

Rebecca's new computer looked awesome, even to Lauren's inexpert eye.

"Nice, Beck," she said.

Rebecca grinned her old grin for a moment. "My parents got the hint. But you know what? They wrapped it anyway. Like I couldn't tell what was inside such big boxes." She shook her head.

"Parents are like that," Lauren said.

"Mine are, anyway," Rebecca answered. Her face got serious again, as if she suddenly remembered she was angry with Lauren. "Sit down," she said. "Let's get to work."

Lauren obeyed. She was grateful for Rebecca's help. But she was even more grateful to be back in the familiar house, sitting near her friend, working on the computer, as they had done so many times before.

Lauren spent Sunday night writing her report. She gave it to Rebecca on Monday morning, who gave it back to her on Monday afternoon with some notes.

Lauren spent Monday night putting the finishing touches on the report and handed it in, in a binder, stuffed full of graphics, graphs, statistics, and footnotes, to Ms. Ivens on Tuesday.

She practically skipped into the rink for her Tuesday afternoon practice session with Annie and Danielle—and stopped short to watch in amazement as Annie did the series of jumps that would finish her long program at the competition. Coach Knudson, who had been Lauren's coach, too, before she recommended Lauren to Eve Perry, said, "Well done, Annie."

Annie bowed, her face flushed with pride.

Coach Knudson turned and saw Lauren. She smiled. "How's it going, Lauren? Is Eve working you hard?"

"Pretty hard," Lauren said. "It's amazing how many times you can do one move over and over."

Coach Knudson laughed. "It's not so amazing if you know Eve. It's good to see you."

She nodded at Danielle and Annie. "Good lesson," she said. "See you tomorrow."

"You did it!" Lauren cried, applauding as

Annie skated toward them. "Annie, that was excellent!"

"Practice," said Annie. She fluttered her eyelashes. "Practice, practice, practice."

"And old movies and pizza," Danielle added. "We had an all-pizza, all-practice weekend. It was awesome."

"I didn't know you planned anything like that," Lauren said, the exhilaration she'd felt from turning in her science report slipping away a little.

"Last-minute," said Danielle. She shrugged. "We would've called, but Annie said she'd talked to you in school and you had some kind of project. We didn't want to tempt you or anything."

Lauren forced herself to smile. "Right. Good thinking." But her smile felt as frozen as a polar ice cap. She bent quickly and pulled on her skates, hoping neither of her friends would notice.

They didn't. They continued to talk at top speed.

"Hey, watch. We developed a new move,"

Danielle said, as Lauren straightened and stepped onto the ice.

"What?"

Annie and Danielle exchanged laughing glances. "I'll show you," Danielle said.

"We call it the pepperoni surprise. We invented it this weekend," Annie said.

Stepping back from the rink's edge, Danielle struck a dramatic pose. Then, planting one foot, she skated in a circle. As she skated, she swayed back and forth. She switched feet and made another circle. This time, she accompanied the swaying by clutching her stomach. At the last moment, she swung around to face Annie and Lauren, dropped to both knees, contorted her face, opened her mouth wide, stuck out her tongue, and hung her head to one side.

"Barf finish," Annie announced. "I'd give it a six."

"I'd give it a *sick*," Lauren said. "That is *so* gross."

"Yeah." Danielle got to her feet. "If you're really nice to us, we'll teach it to you."

"I don't think so," Lauren said.

Abruptly, Annie changed the subject. "So, I've decided on fitted sleeves for my outfit after all. And we're going shopping Friday night to find some new tights. Do you want to come with us?"

"Probably not," said Lauren. "I have a math test on Monday and a science test next Tuesday."

"Evil," commented Danielle. "Hey, guess what?"

"What?" Lauren said.

"Coach Knudson's engaged," Danielle said.

"She has a ring and everything," Annie put in.

Lauren felt a small shock. "When did that happen?" she asked.

"Oh, last week. I meant to call you and tell you, but now you know. We want to get her a great wedding present. Only she hasn't decided when the wedding is."

"Next June," Danielle said. "That's when it should be. She should be a June bride."

"That would be great. It's not in the middle of skating season? I don't think so," Annie scoffed.

Lauren swiveled her head back and forth,

trying to keep up with the rapid volley of the conversation. She felt very left out of things.

"Maybe she'll let us be in the wedding," Danielle went on, ignoring Annie. "After all, we are her students."

"If she lets you, she'll have to let Erica," Lauren said.

"Puh-lease!" Annie made a gagging sound.

"Well, I'm going to start getting ready, just in case. Maybe I'll get a new haircut," Danielle said. "Maybe I'll see if I can talk Mom into a haircut when we go to the mall this Friday to shop for tights."

"Good idea," said Annie. "Hey! We could take our skates and hang out at the ice rink there."

Quietly, Lauren pushed off from the side of the rink and began to glide around it. Annie and Danielle didn't mean to make her feel left out. But Lauren did. While she was trying to catch up in school, their lives were going on—without her.

Ignore it, she told herself. Stick to what's important: skating.

Lauren stopped.

Wait a minute, she thought. It's that kind of thinking that got me into this mess with Rebecca. Skating away from Danielle and Annie isn't going to help our friendship.

And missing Rebecca was teaching Lauren just how important friends were.

Turning, Lauren skated back to join Annie and Danielle. "Hey," she said. "About the pepperoni surprise. Tell me if I'm doing it right."

11

"Rebecca! Rebecca, look at this!" Lauren's voice rose above lunchroom noise.

Lauren had gotten to the lunchroom early and taken a seat at the table in the corner by the window where she and Rebecca always sat. These days, however, Rebecca had been avoiding the lunchroom altogether, and Lauren had found herself with other friends.

But she wished Rebecca would have been there when Lena Lofts, the class president, started talking about the kitten her parents had promised her for her next birthday, or to exchange disgusted looks about Randy's latest gross-out joke.

Today, Lauren waited for Rebecca, determined to catch her before she could eat and run. There she was.

"REBECCA!" Lauren shouted.

Rebecca looked up, startled.

Lauren waved the thick notebook above her head with one hand, and the test paper with the other, a victory flag.

For a moment, Rebecca hesitated. Then she walked over to where Lauren sat and put down her tray. She didn't sit down.

"I got an A– on my paper," Lauren crowed. "*And* Rebecca, check this out—a B+ on my test. I've done it. We've done it. I'll make a B in science this grading period. Is that a miracle, or what?"

"It's not a miracle. It's hard work," Rebecca, ever the practical one, pointed out. "You really worked hard."

"So did you," Lauren said. "Beck, I couldn't have done it without you. You saved me. You saved my whole skating career."

"You did the work," Rebecca said.

"Well, you're the best science coach ever," Lauren said.

Rebecca smiled. "I'm glad. I'm glad you can skate again, too."

"*You're* glad! I'm freaked! I've got a competition in less than two weeks. Every second counts," Lauren said. She paused. "Sit down, if you want. I mean, lunch hour is almost over, so you might as well sit down."

With a glance at her watch, Rebecca nodded. She slid into the seat across from Lauren. "Let me see your test," she said.

Lauren slid the test across to Rebecca, who examined it intently. After a few minutes, she looked up. "Let's go over the problems you got wrong on the test," she said. "It's the best way to learn."

"I don't believe it!" Lauren said. "You want to study? Now?"

Rebecca nodded.

"Okay," said Lauren. "I'll do it. But on one condition."

"What's that?"

"That you come to the competition. It's going to be in Saratoga Springs. At the new rink. It's not even far."

Seeing the look that crossed Rebecca's face, Lauren said, "Or at least promise me you'll *think* about it. Please?"

"Well . . ."

"Please, Beck."

The warning bell rang.

"I'll think about it," Rebecca said.

The Wings' family restaurant was officially closed between 2:30 and 5:00 every afternoon. No cars were parked in the parking lot out front. But Lauren pedaled her bicycle around to the back and propped it against the wall next to the gray metal door that said NO ADMITTANCE.

She opened the door and went down a short hallway into the kitchen. At this hour, it was clean and quiet. She heard her father's voice coming from the freezer, talking to someone about the thermostat.

Lauren crossed the kitchen and opened the door at one end and went up a narrow flight of stairs. At the end of another short hallway, she pushed open a door with the words OFFICE stenciled on it.

"Mom!" Lauren said.

Mrs. Wing looked up from the desk where she sat with a calculator, surrounded by the money and credit slips and checks from lunch.

"Lauren." Mrs. Wing half rose to her feet. "What's wrong?"

"Nothing," Lauren quickly reassured her mother. "It's just that, while you're adding things up, I thought you might like to add this up, too."

Lauren put the report and the test down on the desk by the calculator. Mrs. Wing sat down again and studied the papers. Then she looked up. "Lauren, this is wonderful!" she said.

"I know," Lauren said, grinning. "My grades on my next report card will be, well, back to normal."

"Congratulations," her mother said. "I'm so proud of you."

"Rebecca helped. She tutored me through science. It's because of her that I was able to concentrate on my other subjects, too, without worrying," Lauren said.

"She's a good friend," Mrs. Wing said.

"Yes," Lauren agreed. "The best."

Lauren's mother stood up again. She turned off the calculator and took her purse out of the desk drawer. "Let's get your father. He's downstairs with the assistant manager. I think he should take the night off and we'll have a little celebration."

"Do you also think I can start practicing again after school? The competition is the week after next," Lauren said.

Mrs. Wing put her arm around Lauren's shoulder and gave her a gentle hug. "Oh, I think that can be arranged. Will tomorrow be soon enough?"

12

Lauren finished her spin, turned her head side-ways, and half lowered her eyelids just as the music ended.

Perfect timing. She tried not to breathe too hard, tried to make it appear as if she skated like this all the time. Piece of cake. Nothing to it. Second nature.

"Very well done," said Eve Perry.

Lauren let herself breathe then. The dress rehearsal was over. She smiled at the coach and, gasping for breath, headed for her water bottle.

She drank deeply, being careful not to spill any of the juice and water combination on her outfit.

Day after tomorrow, this huge new arena

would be full of excited skaters, anxious parents, and spectators.

Coach Perry's voice brought her back to the present. "You will have a little advantage, skating in your home rink," Coach Perry said. "You skated with very good feeling. You are more graceful, more balanced."

"It feels that way," Lauren said.

"Good. Good. Now go. I'll see you at the competition." Coach Perry patted Lauren's arm, then stepped off the ice. Lauren leaned against the railing, watching as Eve took off her skates, tucked them neatly into her enormous skating bag, hoisted the tote bag onto her shoulder, and disappeared through one of the arena doorways toward her office.

The rink was quiet now, big and empty. Lauren tipped her head back to stare up at the top row of seats. Would those seats be full? She'd never skated at such an important event before.

She'd never skated at one that had meant so much.

She'd never worked so hard.

Slowly, she glided back out to center ice. She closed her eyes and bowed toward where the judges would sit. She turned and bowed left and right. She imagined the echoes replaced by cheers and applause.

She was ready.

"I'm going to die," Annie said.

"If you need to go to the bathroom, you should go now. There's a huge line," Danielle said. "It took me *hours*."

"It's not that." Annie licked her lips.

Lauren didn't say anything. She had already put on her costume for the short program and now she was waiting. Her heart felt as if it were thumping against the silky material across her chest.

She glanced down. No. Her heart wasn't jumping out of her chest. It just felt that way.

Lauren took a deep breath and watched as Danielle and Annie got ready for the short program. She knew that Danielle would have to make at least two more mad dashes for the bathroom. She knew that Annie would become increasingly grumpy as the time to go on drew nearer.

She watched as Annie's older sister, Moira, smoothed the green-striped skirt of Annie's costume. Moira, solid and calm as a rock, smiled as Annie twitched and tried to peer at the back of her skirt over her shoulder. Standing up, Moira put both hands on her sister's shoulder. "Let's use the mirror," she said, steering Annie toward the long mirror at the end of the row of lockers. "Before you turn yourself into a pretzel."

The noise in the Silver Springs rink wasn't as bad as Lauren was accustomed to in locker rooms at skating events. Maybe it had been designed that way, Lauren thought.

Mrs. Kurowicki sat Danielle down on the bench and began to apply makeup.

Lauren touched her own cheek. She didn't need to go to the bathroom. She'd been ready since she woke up that morning and piled into the car with her family to make the now familiar trip to the Silver Springs rink.

Bryan had plugged into his Walkman. Lacey had claimed the front seat next to their father and spent the trip peering through the window like an explorer. Mrs. Wing, with Lisa sleeping on her shoulder, had closed her eyes.

They'd arrived early and Lauren had given them a tour of the rink where she spent so many hours. Coach Perry, of course, was already there, moving rapidly among the growing stream of arrivals.

When Danielle and Annie arrived, Mrs. Wing turned to Lauren. "Do you want me to stay?"

"No," Lauren said. "I'll be fine."

So now she waited by herself. Even though her friends were nearby, she might as well have been alone on another planet, wrapped up in her own world of anticipation.

Lauren thought of Rebecca. No one had answered the phone the night before. She had no idea whether Rebecca would make it or not, but she'd left a long message with detailed instructions.

More than anything, Lauren wanted Rebecca to be there.

But my family is here, Lauren reminded herself, tracing the edge of the carefully stitched skirt her mother had made. The skirt had an uneven edge, made to flicker just so when it swung out around Lauren's body.

The slightly garbled voice of the announcer came over the speaker in the locker room. One more group and then it would be time for Lauren.

Danielle shrieked and the lipstick her mother was drawing onto her mouth smeared upward. "Oh, *no!*" Danielle cried. "I'll *never, ever,* be ready in time."

"Yes, you will. Hold still," Mrs. Kurowicki ordered, unmoved by Danielle's dramatics.

"I look terrible," Annie said. "Tell the truth, Lauren, because Moira won't. I look terrible."

"You look great," Lauren said. Behind Annie, Moira winked at Lauren.

Moira said, "If you skate as great as you look, Annie, you're there."

"You think so?" Annie said. "Or is this some kind of psychology thing?"

"Either way, I think you should trust us," Moira said. She began to gather up Annie's things, folding garments and rolling socks and tucking them neatly into Annie's skating bag.

Annie thumped down on the bench. "I feel sick," she moaned.

"Well, it'll be a good time to work the pepperoni surprise into your routine then," Lauren said heartlessly.

Annie glared at Lauren, trying to make up her mind to be angry. But she couldn't. Instead, she stuck out her tongue and said, "Thanks for the sympathy," she said. "I'll try to keep it in mind."

"Breathe," Danielle advised, without moving her lips. "Big breaths."

Annie sucked air in through her nose. "Great," she complained. "I just took a big breath of stinky locker room."

Mrs. Kurowicki held up the makeup mirror. Danielle studied her reflection. "Makeup's weird," she said. "I mean, it's face paint. Like a clown, or something."

"You *don't* look like a clown," her mother said. "You look lovely."

She closed the mirror and put it into the makeup kit and began to tidy up, too.

"Good luck all," Moira said. She fluttered

her fingers at them and went up to join the rest of Annie's family.

Mrs. Kurowicki kissed Danielle on the cheek and said, "Give it your best shot. That's what matters." She smiled and nodded at Lauren and Annie, and followed Moira out of the locker room.

The announcer's voice crackled through the air. Lauren, Annie, and Danielle looked at one another. Lauren took a deep breath. "It's time," she said.

13

Lauren and Danielle stood side by side at the edge of the rink, as Annie swept across the ice.

"This is the best she's ever skated," Danielle said softly.

A burst of applause from Annie's family punctuated Danielle's statement as Annie nailed her final jump. Annie's smile was blinding. Her crossovers brought her smoothly back to center and her last spin was so precisely on balance that it left a small pile of ice shavings from the turning blade of the skate.

And then she was done.

The whole auditorium applauded loudly, and

Danielle and Lauren both shouted with delight as Annie skated toward them. Coach Knudson's smile was almost as wide as Annie's and when the scores were held up, it got even bigger.

Annie's eyes widened. "I just beat myself," she announced.

"Your best scores ever," Coach Knudson agreed. "Now drink some water and get some rest. It'll be time for your long program soon." She handed Annie a water bottle.

"After Danielle and Lauren," Annie said. She chugged her water and wiped her mouth. "Can't miss that."

Lauren was the next of the three of them to skate.

As she stepped toward the ice, Coach Perry whispered in her ear, "You know this routine. Go skate with your heart."

For a moment, as she waited to get into position, she forgot to worry as she pondered her coach's words.

Then the music began, and Lauren raised her arms.

The answer to the coach's advice came as she

made her first jump, trying to hang in the air, to fly higher than she or anyone had flown before her.

She was trying to make the jump her own, make people remember how she, Lauren, did it. Make it more than a requirement perfectly done to satisfy the judges.

Who wanted to be just perfect? She skated with her heart, with her love of skating in every move.

She danced her way through the short program, leaping and spinning and pouring all her strength and heart into her skating. On one landing, she felt herself leaning too far back, but she recovered before she could even think about it, and finished triumphantly.

She didn't need the cheers of the crowd to know that she had done well. But one cheering figure caught her eye.

Rebecca. Rebecca, her father, and her mother were sitting in the stands next to Lauren's own family.

Lauren held up both hands and waved, feeling as if she might burst with happiness.

Rebecca gave Lauren two thumbs up, as if she were a movie critic.

After that, Lauren almost didn't care what her scores looked like—until she saw how well she'd done.

"Wow," she said, "I really lucked out."

Eve Perry narrowed her eyes at Lauren. "Talent and hard work, that's your luck," she said. Then, she clapped her hands together. "But it was outstanding skating. Your best so far."

Lauren smiled and then turned.

And there like a snake waiting for a chance to strike was Erica. "Excuse me," she said. "I'm next."

"Good luck," Lauren said, automatically stepping aside.

Erica looked at Lauren with pale, unfriendly blue eyes. "I heard your coach say you skated your best ever. Congratulations."

"Thank you," Lauren said, surprised by Erica's sportsmanship.

"But what are you going to do for your long program, if that was your best?" Erica went on. "Skate your second best? Your third best? Or . . ."

She leaned forward and lowered her voice. "Your worst?"

"I always do my best," Lauren retorted.

Erica gave Lauren a superior smile and stepped out onto the ice.

How elegant she is, Lauren thought in despair—as elegant on the ice as she is mean off of it.

Then a hand yanked at her braid. "Ouch," Lauren said, and turned to see her brother grinning down at her.

"Good job," Bryan said. "You hit 'em low and hard."

"You're mixing up hockey and figure skating," Lauren said, smiling back in spite of herself.

"Whatever," Bryan said. "I'm on my way to get some empty, unnourishing, sugarcoated calories. Want anything?"

"Tell Beck hello for me," Lauren said.

Applause went up as Erica finished her performance. Out of the corner of her eye, Lauren saw a bouquet of flowers go sailing through the air.

"No! Wait," she said to Bryan.

He turned.

"Can you do me a favor? A big, big favor?"

"Depends," said Bryan.

"Meet me outside the locker room door in . . ." Lauren looked at her watch. Danielle still hadn't skated. "In five minutes, okay?"

"I can do that," Bryan said, and sauntered away.

Without waiting to see Erica's scores, Lauren hurried toward her locker. The bouquet of flowers had given her an idea. She hoped she had enough money to make it work.

She got back just in time to watch Danielle skate. She almost wished she hadn't.

The long-legged grace that characterized Danielle's skating didn't hide the glitches in her performance. They weren't big errors: forgetting to point a toe after landing a jump, a moment's traveling in a spin. But with each tiny error, Danielle seemed to get stiffer and stiffer.

"She's skating not to make mistakes," Lauren whispered to Annie, who was clutching her arm.

"I know," Annie said. "Oh, Danielle."

Danielle's back skate had scraped the ice on a landing.

As she came off the ice, Danielle said, "The worst, right?"

"You didn't . . ." Annie began.

"No," Danielle said. "I don't want to talk about it."

"But, Danielle," Lauren tried to speak.

"Later," Danielle said, her voice harsh. "Much later."

She walked down the hall toward the lockers without waiting to check out her scores and without looking back.

14

The minutes ticked by like hours.

Lauren checked and rechecked her costume. She helped Annie stretch. She tried to talk to Danielle, who lay on her back on a bench between the rows of lockers, a towel over her face.

But Danielle wouldn't talk. "I want to be alone," she declared dramatically, her voice muffled by the towel.

And then, much too quickly, it was time for the long program, time for Danielle to jump up and make a mad dash for the bathroom, time for Annie to reknot her sash yet again, time for Lauren to stop pacing among the rows of lockers and tides of restless competitors.

"So soon," Lauren said softly, forgetting how slowly the time had been passing only a moment before.

They went to the rink to wait. Lauren scanned the crowd. Her family was still there. So were Rebecca and her parents.

Lauren turned to watch her competitors, trying to be detached, to learn by watching. But although they were her competition, she rooted for them not to fall, not to make mistakes. Let them skate their best, she said, watching familiar faces and less familiar ones.

And then it was Annie's turn.

"Pepperoni surprise," said Annie in Lauren's ear.

Before Lauren could answer, Annie had stepped out onto the ice.

She smiled a sunny smile as if being in the center of the ice was the only place she wanted to be. She began to skate.

Unconsciously, Lauren's hand gripped Danielle's arm. Beneath her fingers, Lauren felt Danielle's muscles tense as she clenched her hands into fists.

"Go, go, go, go, *go*," Danielle muttered. "Good, good. Ahh, oh, okay, that's okay."

Lauren didn't know Annie's routine by heart as Danielle must have. She had missed so many of the practices and she no longer had lessons with Danielle and Annie. But her heart seemed to be pounding in rhythm to Danielle's voice.

And as if she heard them, as if she felt Lauren and Danielle silently cheering her on, Annie flew across the ice, each move crisp and on beat to the music, each jump steady and precise. When Annie finished, her sunny smile had become an expression of blinding joy.

"You did it, you did it, you did it!" Danielle cried as Annie came off the ice.

"Triple toe loop and a double Axel," Annie breathed as she saw her scores. Clearly, the judges had agreed with Danielle. Now Annie was one of the people to beat in the competition.

"Oh, Annie," said Lauren, hugging her friend hard. Annie hugged her back, and Lauren felt the tremor of her still tense shoulders. "It's okay now, Annie," she whispered. "You can breathe."

"Annie!" It was Moira, followed by the rest of Annie's family. As they engulfed her, Lauren stepped back and saw Erica moving onto center ice.

"No cheers for *you*," Danielle said, staring at Erica. She glanced at Lauren. Of all the people to whom Erica was unpleasant, Lauren was the one who seemed to get the brunt of Erica's dislike.

Lauren shrugged. She couldn't wish bad luck for Erica. She tried not to think about Erica as a person at all, just as a skater.

And as a skater, Lauren saw, Erica was trying too hard. In spite of herself, she drew in her breath as Erica took off on the inside edge of her skate, turning a Lutz into a flip. That would cost her points.

Erica's face showed that she knew it, which in itself could cost her more. As Lauren's coaches had told her ever since she began to skate, you had to keep smiling, had to make it look joyous and natural, even if you made mistakes.

She finished with a layback spin. To Lauren's

eye, Erica's spin was not centered and awkward.

She straightened to applause and Lauren joined in. Two bouquets of flowers came hurtling through the air, big, beautiful bouquets. Erica's parents had thrown them, and Lauren glanced up to see them on their feet, applauding harder even as the rest of the applause died away.

Erica swept up the bouquets and skated off the ice. She straightened after putting on her skate guards and saw her scores.

The judges had seen the lack of finesse in Erica's performance, too. The scores would not be enough for Erica to finish on top.

Tight-lipped with fury, Erica slam-dunked both bouquets of flowers into the trash can and stomped away.

Danielle said to no one in particular, "If she'd been as good on the ice as she was at the flower toss, she might have won."

Lauren looked at the crumpled, broken flowers and felt sad for Erica. Did she feel like that inside? Did she feel as if her life was over? As if her dreams had been thrown away?

That's how I'd feel, Lauren thought.

"Hey," said Annie, coming back to stand beside Lauren and Danielle. She was in her sweats and sneakers.

"Hey, yourself," Danielle said. She grabbed Annie's hand and rubbed her other hand vigorously up and down Annie's arm.

"What are you doing?" Annie said.

"Making some of your skating luck today rub off on me," Danielle answered.

"And my talent," Annie said.

"That, too," Danielle said.

The judge called Danielle's name.

Danielle froze. "I need to go to the bathroom," she croaked.

"No, you don't," Lauren said, giving Danielle a push toward the ice. "You need to go out there and skate like the total ice rocket you are."

"Total ice rocket? Puh-lease!" Danielle said. She rolled her eyes, but she looked less tense. She slipped off her guards and stepped out into the rink.

She skated cleanly, smoothly, flowing from one move into the next. The only flaw that

Lauren saw was a slight posture break on one of her landing positions.

But the judges did not agree. As Danielle surveyed her scores, her shoulders drooped. "I'm out," she said. "That's it."

"Oh, Danielle," said Annie. She took a step toward Danielle as if to comfort her.

Danielle held up her hand. "I really do want to be alone," she said. Her lips were trembling a little as she went on. "Total ice rockets do that when they crash and burn. And I have to go to the bathroom."

She hurried away as fast as she could walk on her blade guards.

Annie turned a stricken face toward Lauren. Lauren swallowed hard. "There's always next year," she said. She didn't know if she was saying it for Danielle or for herself.

They stood in silence at rinkside while the next skater performed her long program.

A touch on the shoulder made Lauren turn. Eve Perry said, "I'll be in the stands where I always am. And you will be on the ice, performing as you always do."

"How is that?" Lauren asked.

"Excellently," said Eve, matter-of-factly. "No less. Empty your mind. Balance yourself in here." The coach made a fist of her small hand and thumped her chest. "That will free your skates to do as they should. Balance."

"Right," Lauren murmured.

"Lauren Wing," the announcer intoned. Far away, Lauren heard a whoop that she knew came from her brother, Bryan.

"There's always next year," Annie said. "But make it this year, okay?" Now it was her turn to give Lauren a push toward the ice.

Lauren smoothed the skirt of her costume. She removed her skate guards. She smoothed the skirt again.

"Go," Annie said.

Lauren went.

Three and a half minutes on the ice, two hundred and ten seconds: such a short time, Lauren thought, as her music began.

The crowd faded into a blur.

Lauren tried not to think of anything at all. She raised her hands.

She began to skate. For a couple of awful steps, a couple of awful seconds, her skates felt leaden. And then, suddenly, as lightly as a stone skipped over water, her feet found their rhythm.

This is easy, she thought. She made a double–double combination and landed perfectly, her head high, her joy evident in her face. With each jump, she gained more confidence. She carved the ice, but lightly, smoothly. When she did her final jump, she truly felt as if she were weightless, as if she were flying.

She landed, perfectly in balance, and finished her program. Only then, as she stood with her arms held high, did she focus on the crowd. Her eyes found her family, all of them on their feet, smiling and cheering. And Rebecca and her parents, too.

Balance, Coach Perry had said.

Balance was everything—in her life—and in her skating.

She heard Annie shouting, "You did it! You did it!"

She saw Bryan's arm go back and then a silver-wrapped bouquet of roses flew high into the air and landed near her. As she picked them up, she felt tears in her eyes. Whatever her score was, she knew she had never skated better.

Bryan was saying something to Rebecca as Lauren cradled the roses and skated slowly off the ice, prolonging the moment, savoring it. Now he was jockeying Rebecca to her feet, half-dragging her down the stairs.

Instead of skating directly back to Annie, Lauren went to the side of the rink at the bottom of the flight of stairs where Bryan and Rebecca were coming down.

Bryan stopped and let go of Rebecca's elbow.

Rebecca's eyes met Lauren's. "These are for you," Lauren said.

Rebecca stepped forward. She looked down at the roses, back up to Lauren. Then her face split into the old familiar grin. She held out her arms and Lauren laid the roses carefully across them.

"Thank you," Lauren said again. "I couldn't have done it without you."

Ever a stickler for accuracy, Rebecca said,

"You probably could have. But it would have been a lot harder."

Then, heedless of the roses, she hugged Lauren hard.

15

Second place.

Lauren couldn't believe it. She'd made it. She looked over at Annie, who had her hand folded over the bronze medal. Annie had come in third.

Antonina Dubonet had come in first. Lauren had skated against Nina before, but not for a long time. She found it hard to recognize the gawky, bony kid she remembered from the year before with the poised, more muscular skater who smiled as the photographer for the local newspaper urged them to move a little closer together.

At the edge of the crowd, Lauren saw her

family and the Meyerses. They were applauding madly, and Lacey and Bryan were fitting their fingers to their lips to let out piercing whistles of celebration.

Coach Perry stood next to Coach Knudson. The two coaches had their heads together. Coach Knudson was applauding as she spoke to Coach Perry. Coach Perry had her hands pressed together in an almost prayerlike fashion, her head tilted to one side to listen as Coach Knudson leaned down toward her. Coach Perry was smiling.

Danielle, Lauren saw, was smiling, too, and some of the happiness seeped away. Danielle wouldn't be going to the next level with Lauren and Annie.

What would that mean? Would Danielle give up her dream of skating, or would she keep going?

Erica, Lauren noticed, was nowhere to be seen.

I'm glad, Lauren thought. She didn't want to think about Erica now, didn't want to watch Erica be a bad sport. She didn't deserve to lose, but even if she had won, to Lauren Erica would never be a winner.

But she wouldn't think about Erica now. If she was lucky, she'd never have to think about Erica again.

The photographer took one last picture, and Annie and Lauren shook hands with Antonina one last time.

"See you soon," Antonina said.

"Yes," agreed Lauren.

Then they were surrounded by their families and friends. Lauren's father enfolded her in a bear hug. "I'm proud of you," he said, his breath tickling her ear. "You earned your place in every way today. You are a champion."

Lauren felt a sudden lump in her throat. She'd almost hated her father and mother for the rules they'd imposed, for not letting her skate as much as she wanted. But she'd been wrong. She hoped they would never know.

She would never let that happen again.

She would always remember to stay in balance, on and off the ice.

Or at least, she would try.

Danielle was hugging her now. "You did good," she said. She stepped back.

"Oh, Danielle," Lauren said.

"I haven't finished," Danielle said. "Keep looking over your shoulder. Because I'll be gaining on you. On both of you."

Annie hugged Danielle. Lauren turned to find Rebecca standing in front of her. She still held the bouquet of roses.

They looked a little limp. Rebecca shifted them in her arms and said, "It's hard to applaud and hold roses at the same time."

"I'm so glad you're here," Lauren said.

"Me, too," said Rebecca. "You're a great skater, Lauren."

"I'm a good skater," Lauren said. "Maybe someday I'll be great."

They smiled at each other. Then Rebecca said, so quietly that Lauren almost didn't hear her, "Actually, I'm a little bit glad you forgot my birthday."

"What?"

Rebecca bit her lip. "Not glad, exactly. But watching how hard you worked, and seeing how much you missed skating . . . I mean, I guess I'd never really gotten it before. Learning something you really don't like learning, just so you can spend hours and hours working in a skating rink."

"It's not work," Lauren said. "Science is work."

"But we had fun working on our science projects." said Rebecca.

Lauren smiled. "Yes we did." Then Lauren got serious.

"I will never, ever forget your birthday again, even when we're a hundred," Lauren vowed. "And I will never, ever forget how important you are to me. You're my BF, big-time."

"You're my best friend, too," Rebecca said. She stuck out her wrist. Lauren looked down and felt her grin stretch so wide it practically touched her ears.

The silver cat bracelet was on Rebecca's wrist.

Lauren looked up. "Nice bracelet," she said.

"Thank you," said Rebecca. "A present. From my BFTS."

"BFTS?" Lauren asked.

"Best Friend the Skater," Rebecca answered.

"I'm hungry!" Danielle shouted. "It's all this

suffering. It's making me starved."

A ripple of laughter met this announcement.

"Let's all go get something to eat," Danielle went on. "Something healthy and good for us, you know . . ."

"NO!" shouted Annie.

" . . . like ice cream," Danielle finished.

More laughter and then Mr. Wing said, "I think I know where we can get some nice, healthy ice cream not far from here."

"Lead the way," said Mrs. Kurowicki.

Mr. Meyers came up. Lauren said, "Can Rebecca ride with us?"

Lauren's mother overheard and said, "We can take Rebecca back home afterward, if you like."

"Fine," said Mr. Meyers. He patted his daughter on the arm. "See you later."

"Double chocolate fudge with triple sprinkles!" Annie let out a whoop and pumped her fist in the air as the crowd began to drift toward the door.

Lauren stopped and looked back at the rink. The stands were emptying out. The ice was opaque with the grooves left by the skaters who had done their best there that day.

"You'll be back," Rebecca said. "With a gold medal, next time."

"I'll be back before then," Lauren said. "I'll be back on Monday morning, five-thirty A.M."

Rebecca groaned and shook her head. "I don't see how you do it," she said, as she had said so often before.

"It's not easy," Lauren said for the first time, instead of laughing it off as she usually did.

Seeing Rebecca's look of surprise she went on, "But it's not hard if you remember to stay balanced about it."

"Five-thirty A.M.? That's *un*-balanced, if you ask me," Rebecca said.

"Balance," Lauren repeated. "It's all about balance, about remembering what's important. Friends. Skating. Family. Skating. Maybe a little science."

"And ice cream," Rebecca said firmly. "You're an ice skating monster, you know that?"

"A total ice rocket," Lauren agreed, and went with her best friend to join her friends and family to celebrate it all.

Ask Michelle!

What is a typical day in your life like?

My day is well planned. I have a regular routine of lessons and practice—three one-hour sessions each day, plus workouts off the ice. All of that has to fit around my college courses, competitions, press interviews, charity work, costume fittings, and—don't forget—a little time to relax and have fun every now and then. I have to be very disciplined to get all this done, of course, but I also have to be very flexible. No two days are the same. No single day is typical. No matter how much you plan, you don't know what's going to happen.

How do you keep up with your schoolwork when you are practicing and competing?

The only way to be a full-time athlete and a full-time student is to be very disciplined. When I was younger, I had to go straight home and study. Starting from when I was in eighth grade, I had a tutor who came to my house every day, but even when she wasn't there, I usually had my nose in a book.

Sometimes even now I feel tired and lazy and tempted to say, "I'll do my homework later." But I quickly learned that *laters* have a way of piling up on each other. It is better just to get the work done . . . and then have some free time!

How do you become an Olympic skater?

It's a long road to the Olympics. The United States Figure Skating Association (USFSA) has eight levels of competitions. When you start out, you're in the Pre-Preliminary level. Then you have to go through Preliminary, Pre-Juvenile, Juvenile, Intermediate, Novice, and Junior before you get to the highest level, Senior. Then you're finally a top skater and eligible for the Olympics.

To make it through all these levels, you must have an overwhelming love for the sport. Then, to get to the Olympics, you need a burning desire—a dream that won't die, no matter what happens along the way. Maybe you'll fall, or lose a competition, or get some criticism, but your dream for the Olympics has to be so strong that nothing could make you give up. And along the way, you have to practice, practice, practice!

Who taught you to skate so well?

I have had so many teachers. My coach, of course, has taught me the most. He's helped me to bring both discipline and artistry to my skating. My choreographer has taught me a lot about how to express my feelings on the ice. Watching other skaters is really important as well. I've studied tapes of the great ones like Dorothy Hamill, Peggy Fleming, Brian Boitano, and Janet Lynn. You don't learn just by doing. You also learn by observing . . . and practicing!

Michelle Kwan, the internationally renowned figure skater, presents

MICHELLE KWAN PRESENTS
Skating Dreams

A new paperback book series about Lauren Wing, a young figure skater, whose hopes and fears, thrills and heartbreaks, closely parallel Michelle's own experiences.

SKATING DREAMS #1:
The Turning Point

SKATING DREAMS #2:
Staying Balanced

SKATING DREAMS #3:
Skating Backward
Coming September 2000

SKATING DREAMS #4:
Champion's Luck
Coming November 2000

Hyperion Books for Children

AVAILABLE SEPTEMBER 2000

Book three in the Skating Dreams paperback series

SKATING BACKWARD

Can she keep it all together or will she be

a secret admirer.
she even has
social life, and
great, she has a
School is going
back in order.
has her life
Lauren finally

Each book
includes Ask Michelle
questions and answers
and a framable
postcard!

Skating Dreams

MICHELLE KWAN PRESENTS